Larina

Book 1 of the Banebridge Companion Novels

A Story in the Soul Forge Universe

Larina by Richard H. Stephens

www.richardhstephens.com

Cover & interior art by: Widget Wyvern Studios

Paperback ISBN: 978-1-989257-27-2

2nd Edition: 2021

Acknowledgements

Larina is the first of three books in the Banebridge Companion Novels, written to complement *Sadyra* and form the basis of book 3, *Pollard.*

While looking to fill in the time between the completion of the Legends of the Lurker series and a research trip* to the British Isles for my next series, The Rise of Grimclaw, I wanted to do something different. I surveyed my loyal readers and asked them which minor character from either of my first two series would they like to see a story written about. Sadyra, the cheeky, fun loving, wear her heart on her sleeve, archer from the Soul Forge Saga was the winner. She beat out notables, Olmar, another favourite from the Soul Forge Saga, Devius Misenthorpe, and Tamra Stoneheart, from the Legends of the Lurker series. I thoroughly enjoyed fleshing out the backstories that explain how Larina and Sadyra came to fight alongside Pollard Banebridge in the Splendoor Catacombs Guard—a division of the Songsbirthian Guard.

*Unfortunately, my research trip has been cancelled due to COVID-19, so the Rise of Grimclaw is now on hold.

On the bright side, as one good thing comes to a halt, another opportunity arises. I am excited to announce the next series in the Soul Forge Universe: Highcliff Guardians. This series will revolve around the elves, Ouderling Wys and Pecklyn Ors, filling in the history with regard to the emergence of the Windwalkers.

Larina is dedicated to one of my biggest fans, Catherine Bogue. Even though you are not a huge fan of the fantasy genre, you have supported and encouraged me right from the beginning, when my debut novella, *The Royal Tournament,* went live. Thank you for your wonderful enthusiasm. It is appreciated more than you know. Don't you ever lose that amazing smile. There will always be a signed copy waiting for you.

None of these stories would be possible without the input of my incredible beta readers. A heartfelt thank you to: Joshua Stephens, Alyssa Gelata, and Caroline Davidson. Your input is priceless.

I would also like to extend a big thank you to my cover and interior picture designer, Tessa Escalera at Widget Wyvern Studios.

Special credit: To honour the Indigenous Peoples of North America, I chose the name Lozen to represent an Altirius Mountain Indian; a title that appears in the original book, *Soul Forge*. All incidents involving Lozen in the books, *Larina*, and *Sadyra*, and *Pollard* are purely fictitious, and by no means represent the real warrior, Lozen.

A brief, unverified history of Lozen.

A famous warrior and prophet of the Chihenne Chiricahua Apache, Lozen was the sister of Chief Victorio.

Born in the 1840s, her brother once said, *"Lozen is my right hand...strong as a man, braver than most, and cunning in strategy. Lozen is a shield to her people."*

Lozen used her spiritual powers in battle; calling on the favour of the gods to discover the location and movement of the enemy.

She participated in many fights on the San Carlos Reservation in Arizona. During those fights, she helped many women and children escape the hands of the enemy and avoided capture herself.

A warrior named Kaywaykla, once said, "She could ride, shoot, and fight like a man; and I think she had more ability in planning military strategy than Victorio."

Lozen fought alongside Geronimo in the last campaign of the Apache Wars.

Going forward.

As in my last series, The Legends of the Lurker, I am always searching for new and unique dragon names. If you wish to submit a name to be added to my list, please connect with me on my Facebook Author Page: RichardHughStephens

Credit in the form of a personal thank you, in the foreword of the book in which the names are used, is my way of giving back to you, the reader. (Including your real name in the acknowledgements will only occur with your permission.)

Zephyr
The Unknown Sea
Mt. Cinder
Mt. Gloom
Cliff Face
Altirius Mountains
Fishmonger Bay
Dragonfang Pass
Thunderhead
Storms End
Frothe River
Redfire Path
The Slither
Zephyr Flats
Forbidden Swamp
Castle Svelte
Madrigail Bay
Carillon
Ring Lake
Saros' Swamp
West Castle Rd
The Forke
Madrigail R.
Millsford
Canorous River
Alpheus' Arch
St. Carmichael's Shrine
Songsbirth
The Spine
The Muse
Niad Ocean
Gritian Hills
Torpid Marsh
Gritian
Treacher's Gorge
Undying Wall
Ghost Island
The Gulch
Lowland Grasslands
Nordic Woods
Nordic Town
Forbidden Pass
The Ocean Way
Redfire Path
Apexceal
Ember Breath

Table of Contents

To view the full colour maps in the Soul Forge Universe, please visit: www.richardhstephens.com

Larina

Book 1 of the Banebridge Companion Novels

A Story in the Soul Forge Universe

Larina

Storms End Lightning Bolt

"**Did** you kill him?"

Larina smiled at the homeless beggar lying in his own filth. Crouching low between vacant buildings, she raised her eyebrows twice. "Danth? Nah. I've something better in mind for him. Let's just say I doubt he'll bother you anymore."

To Larina, life in the cutthroat seaport of Storms End was nothing more than a game of steal and lie, or die. Burnt-out walls of the old city rose up on either side of her crouched form—their desolation instilling in her a strange comfort. A sensation of safety from those she had wronged and planned to con again if she wished to remain alive.

Thunderhead Fjord came to an unemphatic end along the city's polluted shores; slapping its spent energy against countless, rotted pier stanchions lining the haphazard shoreline of the once glorious seaport.

With Thunderhead at the mouth of the fjord, and indeed, the thriving area around Madrigail Bay farther down the coast, Storms End had become little more than a bastion for cutthroat sailors and rogues. A haven for anyone wishing to avoid the attention of the greatest realm the free kingdoms had ever known.

Ruled by a benevolent king, the realm of Zephyr was highly respected amongst her trading partners and enemies alike—a kingdom of tolerance and good fortune. Allies enjoyed the protection of King Malcolm Alexander Svelte, the Learned, while her enemies lay in fear of her mighty war machine.

At least they had before Helleden Misenthorpe returned from the dead and laid waste to the kingdom. The rumour circulating around the city was that Zephyr had lost the ability to defend itself. If the ‘so-called’ benevolent King Malcolm didn’t get his act together soon, there might not be a kingdom left to save. Larina had heard rumblings of the Kraidic empire gearing up for war whispered in the dark corners of taverns and places of ill-repute.

Those rumours were unsettling. For those left alive in the ancient shipbuilding city in the aftermath of the maniacal sorcerer’s invasion two years ago, and the subsequent death of their much beloved queen, Quarrnaine, life had never returned to normal. Many were left homeless or without family. Larina couldn’t imagine how bad things would become if Zephyr were invaded again. The Kraidics were notorious seafarers—brutal and relentless when they had an enemy in their sights.

As was the case for the spirited lass known to anyone undesirable enough to have the misfortune of making the acquaintance of the Storms End Lightning Bolt. Larina cared less for the title she had been given; preferring to remain nameless and faceless to facilitate her penchant of slipping from shadow to shadow unmolested by the authorities. For her, survival had been inbred at an early age.

Gazing at the end of the alley where she knew they would come, the weak voice of the elderly man she helped prop against a charred wallboard drew her attention.

“You must go. I’ll be okay. They won’t bother with the likes of me when they’re on the hunt.”

She gave him a compassionate smile, her long cheeks lifting on the ends of thin lips. Flicking a loose strand of brown hair from in front of her face, she adjusted the filthy burlap sack around the frail man's shoulders. "I'll be back, Allard, don't worry. When I return, my bag will be stuffed with food."

She could tell by Allard's eyes that his time to leave this world wasn't long in coming. The fact that he suffered so, this close to the end of his life, raised her hackles.

Allard had spoke of him once being an important man in the king's army. If she believed half of the tales he had imparted during the several, cold nights she had snuggled next to him over the last couple of years to share body warmth, he had played an important part in the Battle of Lugubrius two decades ago.

As delighted as the haggard man sounded of his accomplishments, he never told Larina what exactly he was proud of. At first, she had put it down to the ramblings of an old man, but the more she came to know him, the more she began to believe his tales.

She patted his shoulder and stood, adjusting the belt holding her black tunic against her thin waist.

Allard reached out but didn't have the strength to bend forward. "Promise me you'll get yourself a better weapon. A dagger's fine if all you want to do is sneak up behind someone and cut their neck, but with the enemies you're acquiring, it won't be enough to keep you safe."

She blinked as his words sunk in. Pulling her nondescript dagger from its sheath, she bent at the knees and waggled it between them. "Good ol' '*stick 'em*' has served me fine so far. You needn't fear, my old friend. Pray for the families of those who chase me."

She stood, sheathed her dagger, and padded quietly in her soft-soled boots to peer out of the end of the alley.

Larina

It took her a moment to find them. Coming down a broken, wooden plank walkway fronting the remains of the old section of town, several large figures made their way toward her hiding spot. She jumped back to Allard and took hold of the burlap—pulling it over his head.

"They're coming. Best you don't draw attention to yourself." She inspected the darkness at the far end of the alley and took a deep breath. "Be safe, old boy."

She ran halfway down the dark backstreet and stopped in the shadows. Something didn't feel right.

Born from the one-time bond of her mother and a paying customer, Larina's first memories were of being left alone to fend for herself in a warren of shanties and derelict buildings—the resulting fallout of the same maniacal sorcerer's sojourn into Zephyr twenty-one years prior.

During the many nights that her wayward mother would return smelling of stale smoke, ale, and something more repulsive, she would find Larina huddled in a corner, shivering with fear. More often than not, her mother would berate Larina's weakness before passing out in preparation of beginning the cycle all over again whenever she awoke the next day.

On the odd occasion, her mother, out of what Larina now suspected must have been guilt, offered her sympathy. She claimed Larina was the daughter of a high-born sailor whose ship had docked in Storms End.

Larina swallowed, fighting to keep her eyes from misting over in the dangerous alleyway. Many were the sleepless nights she had lain alone, listening to night sounds; scrabbling, scratching, clawing, and shouting all around her. The only thing that had helped her survive the night terrors was the misplaced belief that one day her father would return and take her away from a life of squalor.

She had held onto that belief until the day she heard rumours that her living space in the one-roomed hovel she shared with her mother was about to be 'vacated.' A term she had become well versed in. 'Vacated' signified that the owner had either died or moved on.

At the age of nine, she had been forced to reconcile the fact that her mother was not coming back. Her time in their flea-infested living space had come to an end. Perhaps more grievous than the report of her mother's impending demise, was the death of her dream. Once her mother was gone, the highborn sailor would have no reason to return.

She had rushed to the seedy district her mother frequented and found her sprawled in a back alley amongst piles of refuse, her clothing soaked in blood. Not knowing whether to scream at her mother for being so careless, or to cry, she held her dying mother's cheeks between her hands and demanded to know the truth about her mysterious father.

With the last of her strength, her mother had shrugged. The words uttered on her dying breath haunted Larina to this day. *'Who knows? It may be true. Why not hang onto that vision. It's probably the best thing I've ever given you.'*

Movement at the head of the alley startled her out of her memories. Wiping at her eyes, it was time for the Storms End Lightning Bolt to run.

Larina

Rooftop Romp

Movement at the opposite end of the alley kept Larina crouched behind a pile of empty crates. She had no way of knowing whether the people chasing her had split up, but she couldn't afford to find out. She thought that she should probably stop taking such drastic measures to keep people like Allard safe from the ever-present predators but she couldn't do anything about it now. Frightened by the realization that if they caught her, those she assisted would be left without protection, she searched for a means to escape.

The area reeked of urine. Across the alley, a small rat skittered into the moonlight, sniffed at the air, squeaked, and waddled into the shadows; disappearing through a crack in the wallboards. If only it were that easy.

The people from the street stopped at the alley entrance and took an interest in the pile of burlap.

Her breath came in ragged spurts. Eyes narrowed, she stepped from the shadows, her gaze flitting from one end of the alley to the other.

Gathering strength from the deep-rooted reserve she had acquired by virtue of her upbringing, she stared at the group inspecting Allard's resting place. "Cowards! Why don't you pick on someone capable of fighting back?"

Larina

Though hard to see in the poor light, it was obvious she had gotten their attention. Someone kicked out at the burlap before they followed their companions into the alley.

She gritted her teeth, trying to identify the person responsible for kicking out at Allard. If she ever discovered who it was, she would use her dagger the way Allard had mentioned—except she wouldn't sneak up from behind. She had no qualms about meeting anyone head on. A trait her few friends around the city told her would be the death of her.

Taking a deep breath, she flexed her fingers; preparing herself mentally for what she had to do.

What remained of the crumbling building at her back was only a single story. The leaning building across the narrow alley rose into the darkness for at least two. Fist raised at the people who had lashed out at poor, defenseless Allard, she ran at the wall of the higher building; crouching and leaping at the suspect wallboards.

Her feet scrabbled momentarily as she grasped the edges of separated boards above her head. Cat-like, she sprung across the alleyway and hit the lower building's wall at head level with enough force to spring back across to the taller building, and back one more time. Her momentum waned, but it was enough.

She hung by her hands from the precarious eave for a moment. Scanning both ends of the alley, she confirmed that her pursuers had indeed split up, and were closing in fast.

No sooner had she heard a crossbow release, the bolt thumped into the wallboard beside her waist, giving her that little bit of added incentive to hoist her body over the jagged eave and out of sight. Her movement caused a large bird perched on the roof's edge to takeoff.

Larina

"You can't hide forever, Bolt!" A deep voice she recognized all too well followed her into the night. "Running won't save your friend!"

She stopped, perched on the edge of a hole in the rooftop and looked back at where she had ascended. She wasn't overly concerned that anyone had the ability to follow her up the wall—not many people could match her agility. Clasping the hilt of her dagger, she considered going after the group but thought better of it. She wasn't afraid to face multiple targets but she wasn't naïve either. Dying in the alley tonight served no one.

Swallowing the guilt rising from the pit of her stomach, fearing for Allard, she refocused her survival instincts. It wouldn't be long before her pursuers found their way to the rooftop. She sprinted around the gap and ran for the far eaves.

Several more holes riddled the derelict structure's rooftop—beams twisted and fallen into its bowels. Leaping across a wide gap, she momentarily feared she'd miscalculated her jump, but landed safely on the torn lip of splintered wood. She wind-milled her arms, barely preventing herself from falling backward before crouching low and steadying herself with her hands.

Noise from within the building attracted her attention. She recognized the three men but the presence of a woman she'd never seen before almost cost Larina her life as she paused to take a closer look at the darker skinned female.

The lead man, Danth Emerald, someone she had grown up with until he had joined the Watch, raised a loaded crossbow, aimed, and released the latch. The bolt whistled through the gap, shattering the edge of the rim it braised; at minimum, a disabling shot if Larina hadn't reacted as fast as she had.

Larina

A squeal of fright escaped her lips. She missed a step and stumbled to the edge of the roof. Instead of risking falling into the alley below, she sprung wildly across the gap and crunched into a ball; covering her face with her arms as she crashed through a tall window comprised of many smaller panes.

A brown-furred cat shrieked and scrabbled for purchase on the dirty hardwood floor, kicking up bits of garbage on its way through an open doorway.

Two elderly people looked up from where they huddled together in a corner by the doorway. If Larina's tumultuous entrance had startled them, it didn't show on their haggard faces.

She rolled to an ungraceful stop. Rising to a single-kneed crouch, she carefully pulled the shards of glass and splintered wood from her clothing. Blood seeped from several small cuts, but they were nothing to be concerned about given her current state.

She slunk over to the edge of the window and peered out—pulling back again in time to miss being hit by an arrow that shattered part of the remaining section of window she hadn't taken into the room with her. The arrow punctured the wall opposite the elderly couple.

With her back to the wall, Larina slipped around the inside of the room toward the door; stopping to address the vacant stares watching her. "Sorry about that."

She took a few moments to inspect the couple. Not able to recall seeing them before, she surmised they must have been driven out of their home recently—likely due to an inability to pay their rent. She smiled at them for their sake. They were both alive, but appeared in worse shape than Allard.

She patted the woman on the shoulder. "Are you two okay?"

A subtle nod from the elderly male was the only reply she received.

Reluctantly getting to her feet, she made a point to come back and check on them after she had eluded the Watch.

The noise of boots hammering up a flight of steps grabbed her attention. She took a deep breath and held it—diving across the threshold to roll into the foyer beyond as a crossbow bolt and another arrow clattered off the wonky balustrade lining the head of a wide staircase spiraling down to the floor below.

Larina wasn't certain, but she doubted the lower floor was the ground floor. Storms End was built on the steep slopes rising out of the seemingly bottomless fjord.

Her back against the foyer wall, she looked over her shoulder to ensure the window she had crashed through wasn't visible. Knowing her time was running out, she sprinted along the wall, past the staircase, and through another open doorway into a room littered with broken furniture. Another arrow clattered by her feet and bounced off the doorjamb—coming to a rest against a heap of discarded blankets. Someone squatted here as well, but whoever they were, they weren't around at the moment.

A window, matching the one she had broken, lined the far end of the room, admitting light from the three-quarter moon hanging over the fjord far below. Ships of all sizes dotted the shoreline—skeletal spars and masts strung together with hawsers casting eerie shadows on the flickering water and pale buildings lining the bay.

Many were the day that Larina had sat on the end of a pier, waggling bare feet above the brackish water and dreaming of her father's boat sailing in to whisk her away—billowed sails cast in a golden hue as a brilliant sunset heralded its arrival.

Larina

Footsteps pounded on the stairs leading up to the floor she was on. She didn't have time to waste on an unfounded dream. She would be no good to the old couple dead. Unlatching the window, she opened the two panels of grimy windows and vaulted onto the spacious sill. Thankfully the next building's rooftop sat lower than where she perched. From her vantage point, she mind-mapped a route that would take her across the broken buildings and down to the old part of the city closer to the harbour.

She had fled in this manner many times during the past couple of years. Sooner or later, those giving chase would get wise and team up to pin her in. A few, well placed sentries hiding on the rooftops were all it would take to end her game of dragon and troll. Tonight, she prayed she would evade the dragon and escape to the one area her presence was welcome.

The cold night air felt good wafting through her fine hair as she leaped to the adjacent building. Every time she landed, she dropped to a crouch. More than once a rooftop had given way beneath her. This rooftop held. Running across the flimsy surface, she trusted her bearings—a mighty leap carried her across a narrow street.

Every time she jumped, she was positive her heart skipped a beat. The uninviting cobblestones far below promised an excruciating outcome should she ever miscalculate.

A steep slope comprised the peak of the next building, making for a surprisingly easy landing. The trick on these types of slopes was to keep solid contact with the soles of her boots—resisting the urge to scrabble in fear of slipping. The loss of contact with any part of her hands or boots opened up gravity's penchant to assert its hold and pull her toward an unfortunate demise.

Larina

Two buildings back, two silhouettes vaulted in unison to the roof she had just vacated—the billowing hair of the lead person could be none other than that of the unknown woman. Someone deserving further investigation. The seriousness of the newcomer's presence was offset by the fact that only two people had managed to remain on her heels.

Larina so enjoyed the thrill of the flight. Locating a handhold, she pulled herself up to the ridgeline and swung her legs ahead of her. With her back to the steep slope, she let her momentum pull her down the far side; her attention momentarily distracted by the flight of what appeared in the darkness to be a small hawk.

Timing was everything when it came to rooftop hopping. Jump too early and your leap fell short. Leave it too late, especially when sliding down the steeper inclines, and you risked dropping over the eave before you leaped. Larina's timing was perfect.

She landed hard—the next rooftop clearly a full story lower. Her forward momentum carried her into an unorthodox summersault. She paused long enough to ensure her dagger remained firmly within its sheath, and made her way around the protruding chimney tops to the far side of the building.

An arrow bit into the rotten wood beside her.

She couldn't believe her eyes. Perched on the crest of the steep rooftop, waist-length hair billowing in the breeze behind her, the mystery woman strung another arrow. Of her partner, Larina couldn't see what had happened to him.

Not waiting to find out how proficient the archer was, Larina leaned back to gather momentum and launched herself to the balcony of the tall building that stood in her way. She landed inside a fancily carved railing but she had no time to admire the ancient woodwork. Grasping the smooth railing with one hand, she threw her legs over the side and dropped to the balcony below—repeating the procedure two more times before she landed quietly on the damp cobblestone street and sprinted down an adjacent alley.

The streets were her home. Once in the clear, she never doubted her ability to evade anyone that might be chasing her, but something about the persistence of the archer gave her pause.

Street corner after alleyway passed by in a rush. She never took the same route twice. Up one alley, over a retaining wall and recklessly clambering down a hill too steep to build on. She dared not return to the rooftops of the buildings closer to the water. If the archer remained on her trail, she would be spotted.

As the embankment levelled out, she sprinted across a wide bridge. Ancient stone buildings lined the canal road on both sides; separating the fjord and the rank aqueduct fronting the city proper. Curious stares from dark alcoves followed her progress but no one made a move toward her. She recognized a few faces that smiled after her, whispering words of encouragement, "Go, Lightning Bolt, go."

Looking over her shoulder many times, she couldn't detect any sign of pursuit, but her street-smart education had taught her not to let her guard down. She had been on both ends of the chase too many times to count—the hunted and the hunter. It didn't pay to become complacent.

Her rapid, short strides carried her around the end of the bay and along the southern leg of Canal Road. It wasn't until she slammed against the side of a familiar stone wall that she dared to let her guard down. The *Kraken's Curse* felt reassuring against her side as she bent over to catch her breath.

Larina

"Out for an evening stroll, Bolt?" A nasally voice sounded behind her from the direction of the canal.

Startled, she straightened, spun, and brandished her dagger at a middle-aged man; barely restraining herself from plunging it into his chest.

"Easy, lass. You're amongst kindred spirits." The balding, pepper-grey haired man held up his palms in a non-threatening manner.

Larina lowered her dagger and cocked her head sideways, releasing a deep sigh. "Damn you, Rock. I could've killed you."

"Could have tried." He flashed a gapped-tooth smile, raising his eyebrows.

A filthy, straight pipe appeared in his hand. He chomped on its narrow end and struck a flint with a small blade over its corncob bowl until he got it smoking. Drawing deeply, the bowl illuminated his face in an orange glow. "If you *had* tried, you'd find yourself at the bottom of the canal."

Larina shook her head and sheathed her dagger. She had no qualms about Rock's ability to back up his bravado. He never carried a weapon other than the small blade he used to light his pipe, but she had never seen him lose a fight.

There weren't many who would so much as look at Rock the wrong way. Scrawny and not very handsome—an old scar marred his left cheek, not far below his eye—his pock-marked appearance didn't do the dangerous nature of the man justice, but she knew better. Had he followed through with his casual threat, she wouldn't be the first person to end up on the bottom of the canal at his hands.

"Looks like someone tried to kill you," he said, casually studying the cuts she had received leaping through the window. "Who'd ya irritate tonight?"

Larina smiled for his benefit and peered around the corner of the *Kraken's Curse*. The streets were empty to anyone who didn't know what to look for. She located several people standing or skulking about the shadows, but none of their movements alarmed her. Not many souls would hazard the streets this late at night unless they were well-armed or travelled in numbers—or were deliriously drunk.

Trolls were often a nuisance in the upper section of the city but down by the water they were the least of a wary person's concern.

She pulled back and raised her eyebrows as if that answered Rock's question.

"Hmph." He puffed on his pipe, blowing a great waft of smoke upon the cold air. "Get yourself into the *Curse* and warm your hide. I'll see that no one makes it past here."

"Thanks, Rock. I owe you one."

Rock's eyes never left her as she grasped the thick handle of the only doorway into the *Kraken's Curse.* "One? Pfft. More like a few dozen."

She stopped with the door half open. Yellow rushlight spilled onto the cobbles on the wake of a blast of welcome warmth. She didn't know a lot about the hardened man's past—he was never forthcoming when it came to talking about himself—but she knew from the words they had shared that his life had not been an easy one. Nor had she ever seen him in the company of a woman, which suddenly struck her as odd.

A heartfelt twinkle filled her eyes as she spoke over the unintelligible din escaping the tavern. "Someday you'll make a maiden happy."

"Hah!" Rock slapped his pipe bowl on his thigh—sparks and ash spilling over the permanent stain on his brown leather breeks. “I’m past my lassie chasing days. Get inside and tend to your hurts before I change my mind.”

Larina laughed and pulled the heavy door shut behind her.

Larina

Whispered Rumours

Boisterous laughter, loud voices and clinking tankards resonated within the large common room of the *Kraken's Curse*—a smoky haze lingered in the warm glow of flickering sconces. The din hushed momentarily as Larina stepped inside, but upon seeing her, most people returned to their own business.

A burly man, his face hidden behind a thick, black beard, perked his head up from a table along the middle of the wall opposite the bar. "Over here, lassie!"

All at once, Larina felt the stress ease from her taught muscles—washing away the anxiety that accompanied her nightly endeavours. The presence of the man, known to everyone as Bear, filled her soul with a sense of calm. Though he may not be able to stand up against the likes of Rock, there wasn't anyone else in the entire world that she'd rather be with than the brother of her slain, childhood friend. Bear's sister had been her only friend while growing up. How she missed sweet Cassie.

She smiled ruefully at her dear friend's memory, and made her way through the throng to Bear's table. She had no idea who the three men were sitting across the table from him, but she didn't care.

Ten years older than Larina, she couldn't remember the last time she had spoken Bear's real name. In the circles they travelled, real names meant trouble.

Larina

"What did you do now?" Bear asked sliding his bulk out from the table. He motioned for a barmaid to give up the cloth she carried.

"Same old." Larina took the cloth and dabbed at her scratches; holding the cloth against the deepest cut on the back of her hand. For the most part, the blood had already crusted over all but the worst of her hurts.

In spite of her discomfort, she accepted Bear's meaty embrace; the folds of his body enveloping her like a duvet. Ignoring the reek of sweat, she hugged him back—her hands unable to touch as she fought to keep him from squeezing the air from her lungs. "I can't breathe, you big lug."

"Hah!" He squeezed her tighter, eliciting a gasp, and then let her go; his rosy cheeks visible above his beard. "A better way to die ain't never been invented, Bolt. You remember that when the time comes."

She slugged him in the shoulder, her hard punch slapping leather armour. Cupping her fist, the blow hurt her more than him. She doubted he felt it at all.

"Oi! One of these days I'll have you over me knee." Bear winked at the three tough-looking brutes sitting across the table.

"Cheers to that!" The largest man said and clanked sloshing tankards with his mates.

Unperturbed, Larina snatched Bear's drinking vessel from his hand, clanked it with the others and downed its contents.

The three strangers exchanged glances as she slapped the tankard on the table and belched loud enough to make a hardened sailor proud.

The men spit their mead through clenched mouths, unable to withhold their amusement.

Bear shrugged. "This is the woman I was telling you about."

The men nodded and wiped their mouths with dirty cuffs.

"Gentlemen, meet the Storms End Lightning Bolt. If there's something you be needing but not sure how to get your hands on, Bolt is the one to talk to."

The men bowed their heads in acknowledgement.

She gazed into each man's eye, lingering long enough to show them she wasn't cowed by their appearance. Dropping the last man's gaze, she spun and held her hand high, snapping her fingers at a busty serving wench. When the barmaid looked her way, Larina held up six fingers.

Bear resumed his seat. "You look flummoxed, lass. What've you been up to tonight, or should I be asking?"

"Move over." Larina slapped at the rolls hanging over Bear's thick belt and slid onto the bench beside him. Wrapping her dainty fingers around this massive forearm she gazed into his brown eyes. "Up top seeing to our elders."

The smile left Bear's face. "Ah. Of course."

"Allard's in a bad way."

"Only a matter of time for that one."

His affirmation of her fear for Allard's failing health stoked her fires. "It's time I step it up."

"Easy, lassie. You're only one person. You can't save the world."

"I came across a new couple tonight. A man and woman I've never seen before. They look in worse shape than Allard. The baron's brutal policies to clean up the upper tiers lack compassion. Who's going to help them? They can't fend for themselves."

Bear raised his eyebrows, nodding as she spoke. "Aye. As I said before, it may seem hardhanded to people like us, but who are we to know whether those in power are purposely negligent to the lesser folks—"

Larina

"Who are we?" Larina's breaths came in short, heavy gasps. "How do you explain throwing Allard into the streets so they can rip down a building *those in power* don't care for any longer? Is that the way our less fortunate should be treated? From what I understand, Allard was some kind of hero in the king's army. Someone who gave everything for our kingdom. Now he freezes in the streets with an empty stomach. That's our way of saying thanks? It's downright cruel."

Bear bit his thick lips, shaking his head. "I can't explain why our leaders to do what they do. No, there's no excuse for tossing people to the trolls, and I agree, it doesn't make a lick of sense." He held up a sausage-like finger to cut her off. "But, what you're doing, as noble as you think it is, isn't helping their cause."

"How can you say that?" Larina gasped, releasing his arm. "If not for me, Allard and many more would starve to death."

Bear nodded patiently.

"If not for me, they would *freeze* to death. Autumn isn't far off. It'll arrive on the breath of winter's gales before we know it, and then what? We can't just sit back and wash our hands of them."

Bear clasped her hands in his, engulfing them as if hers belonged to an infant. "Bolt. I agree with everything you say. You know I do. But you also know how I feel about striking back at the system."

She tried to wrest her hands free, but couldn't. "Ya. You'd rather let them have their way and hope that this will all go away. You and everyone else would rather—"

Bear's face darkened. His raised voice drowned her out. "You know full well where my loyalties lie. Don't even go there." He released her hands.

Larina

Larina stood up, her face scrunched in outrage. It was all she could do not to spit. How had their conversation gone sideways so fast?

"What you can't wrap your pretty little head around is what's really happening here."

She glared at him, knowing what he was about to say. He had said as much before.

"Your actions, noble as they may be, have upset the city Watch. By doing so, the baron has reacted in a way that is detrimental to those you work so hard to protect."

Deep, hungering breaths escaped Larina's flaring nostrils. Had Bear been anyone but her dead friend's brother, she would have stuck him with her dagger for insinuating her actions had made matters worse. The fact that what he said made sense in a crazy, roundabout way, did little to mollify her resentment. It maddened her to the point that she screamed, "And just what do *you* think we should do about it?"

The noise in the busy barroom fell off so abruptly, a cold chill crept along her skin. The odd clink of someone putting a dish down and a couple of people clearing their throats were the only sounds that reached her reddening ears. Fit to be tied, she glared around the room, talking as she did so. "What are you looking at? Mind your own business."

A few grunts and unintelligible grumblings met her glowering attention. As she turned back to Bear and the three men she hadn't met before, the din in the tavern resumed its former level, but Larina felt eyes watching her. That wasn't good. She lived by the code of *not* attracting attention. Though most knew her nickname, few knew much else.

Bear motioned for her to sit. "Bolt, it doesn't do anyone any good if you and I disagree on how we can best help them.

Fundamentally, we're on the same side." He patted the bench. "Come."

She stared hard into his big eyes; releasing two, long breaths. Casting the three strangers an intense look, she retook her seat, but didn't wrap her hands around Bear's forearm.

The barmaid approached; a large tray laden with overflowing mugs balanced in one hand. Larina placed seven coppers in the servant's free hand, accepted the first two tankards, and indicated the rest were for the men. As the barmaid handed the last mug to Bear, Larina plopped an empty one back on the tray.

"I don't know where you put it." Bear said, holding up his tankard. "Truce?"

Larina glared at him for a moment longer for good measure. "Truce."

Amused by their ramblings, the three men looked as if they were afraid to interrupt, but they clanked their mugs in toast of a truce.

Larina knocked back half of her second mug in one, fluid swallow. Banging it on the table, she forced a smile for the three dangerous looking men. "And who do we have here?"

"Typical Bolt. Straight to the chase." Bear laughed. "Pardon the pun." He looked around the table but was met with blank stares.

He cleared his throat. "Well, anyway. Bolt, these fine gentlemen are looking to hire someone of your…particular talent."

She wasn't impressed. Many people sought out her skills, but most didn't possess the means to pay up front. They promised her compensation when the job was complete. She had been burned more than once by entering into such an arrangement. Doing business on those terms, she might as well just do the job for herself and keep all of the reward.

"And are these...*gentlemen*...capable of paying ahead of time?"

She gave Bear a bored look, but was surprised when the thinnest man of the three responded.

"We're prepared to pay you a hundred gold pieces upfront and another three hundred if you are able to pull it off." He looked across the chiselled features of the man in the middle toward the biggest man sitting against the wall. "Show her, Tiny."

If she hadn't been so shocked by the sum they were willing to pay, Larina doubted she would have been able to supress an urge to laugh. The man referred to as Tiny was easily six-foot-eight and nearly as wide. His bulk made Bear appear thin.

Tiny produced a fair-sized leather satchel and opened its drawstring; casting a wary eye around the barroom as he did so. He leaned his massive arms across the table; the contents of the bag chinking as he set it in front of her.

Larina caught a glimpse of the coins and frowned. "There's more than a hundred in there." She reached out to run her fingers through the loot, but Tiny pulled it away, his high-pitched voice sounding peculiar in a man of his size. "Uh, uh. Listen to Cyello, first."

"Thank you." The thinnest man, who was by no means skinny, smiled at Tiny. "You have keen eyes. Your entire payment is there."

Immediately her mind went to what she could buy with four hundred gold pieces. If she hadn't stolen the odd one here and there, she would never have held one in her hands. Visions of purchasing one of the bigger, more intact buildings in the upper tiers and converting it into living spaces for all the homeless and less well-to-do of Storms End raised goosebumps along her arms. She could furnish them and still have money left over to feed them.

Her face contorted from one of wonder to a skeptical sneer. If they had that much money, what did they need her for?

"You don't think that's enough?" Cyello asked, raising his eyebrows at Bear.

She swallowed and sputtered, "Why, yes. But if you have so much money, what do you need me for? You can buy whatever you want."

Cyello's face became serious. "What we want can't be bought."

Her brows furrowed. She couldn't stop her eyes from flitting to the meanest looking man who sat in the middle; the head of a black warhammer poking over his shoulder. "Look. I'm not afraid to kill anyone, but if you're looking for an assassin—"

"An assassin? No, we deal with such things on our own."

"Then what? What can be worth four hundred gold?"

Cyello tried to hush her by motioning with downturned palms. He and his men searched the crowd.

Larina did likewise, a flush of embarrassment warming her cheeks, but nobody appeared to take an interest in their conversation. She leaned over the table. "What's so important that you're willing to part with so much coin?"

Quiet until now, the man with the warhammer sighed. He patted Cyello's nearest hand. "Allow me."

Cyello nodded and sat back.

Though he looked menacing, studying his chiselled features, Larina thought he was actually the most pleasant in appearance of the three ruffians.

He leaned forward to meet her face-to-face. Displaying a set of perfect teeth, his stunning green eyes held her stare.

"You ask a lot of questions for a thief. Perhaps we've been negligent in allowing our mutual friend," he dipped his head at Bear, "to convince us that you're the person best suited to our needs. You have to admit, at first glance, you aren't an intimidating sort." He raised his eyebrows twice, a forced smile twitching the corners of his mouth. "At least not from a confrontational point of view."

She frowned, her dander rising. "Your needs? If you're after a patsy, then you're right. Go find someone else to talk down to. *But!*" She pointed a finger at the man's dimpled chin. "If you're looking for a job done right and without a trace, then watch your mouth or I'll shove those coins into places you'd rather I didn't get to know. Is that clear?"

The man leaned back, not taking his eyes off her. He folded corded forearms below his thick chest and nodded. "Perhaps I'm hasty to judge the Lightning Bolt, hmm?"

Larina held his stare for a few moments longer before leaning back and grabbing hold of her tankard—finishing it in a single pull.

Bear smiled down at her with admiration. "Well, Korwynn? If she's half as good as she can quaff a mug, I'd say you've found the one you're looking for."

She shook her head. "Not until I find out what you're after. I may be good, but I'm not stupid."

Korwynn considered her a moment. Catching the eye of the barmaid he motioned for another round and waited to speak until after he flipped the overjoyed woman a silver coin for her troubles.

He lowered his voice. "Are you aware of the Banebridge homestead?"

Larina nodded. Who wasn't? "The one perched over the fjord above Storms End?"

"That's the one."

"I know *of* it, but someone as lowborn as myself has never had the opportunity to visit."

"How would you like to know it intimately?"

"The home of the Kraidic Crusher?"

As one, the three men took in a deep breath.

"What? Surely, you're not afraid of Thoril the Kraidic Crusher? He died years ago. His son, Thoril Half-Hand, still lives there as far as I know, but he's as old as the fjord is deep."

Korwynn cleared his throat. "*We're* not afraid of the man, but he holds something that doesn't belong to him."

"Ah, you're after a possession. What? A tapestry? Sculpture?"

"A scroll."

Larina choked on a mouthful of mead. She searched each man's face, trying to read something from their serious stares. An inexplicable, uncomfortable feeling feathered its way down her back—as if her life hung in the balance, depending on her reaction. Swallowing the silliness of the notion, she leaned in, her gaze darting about the tavern. Absently wiping at the drool dripping down her chin, she asked, "A scroll?"

Korwynn dipped his chin.

"Is it magical?"

Korwynn's voice belied his dark glare. "In and of itself…" He shrugged and ran his tongue along the inside of his upper lip. "If you're worried it'll harm you, I assure you, it won't."

"Then why would an ordinary piece of parchment command the price you offer."

The irritated look Korwynn flashed Bear wasn't lost on her. He returned his attention to her; the threat of malice strong behind those green eyes. "Do you want the job or not?"

Larina

There was definitely something intrinsically wrong about what the man was asking her to do. Something sinister, if she had the right of it. It took every bit of nerve she possessed to hold his menacing stare as she debated the merits of what he proposed.

Thoril Banebridge was perhaps the most respected man living along the entire west coast of Zephyr. When people spoke of him it was like they spoke about someone in the royal family. Who knew? Perhaps he was. Thoril's father, labelled the Kraidic Crusher, had been instrumental in driving out the invading Kraidic army long before she had been born. If she remembered correctly, the elder Thoril had disappeared in the lofty mountains lining Zephyr's northern shore and was never heard of again.

There was also the matter of Thoril Junior being the Master of the Storms End council. Though not the baron, his authority carried almost as much clout as the Chambermaster of the Wise. If she was caught breaking into such a prestigious household, her life would be forfeit.

She sighed and sat back, breaking the man's glare. She stared at her folded hands on the table, gently shaking her head. There was no way.

Korwynn threw back his mead. "Come on, boys. Ain't nothing to be gained here."

Bear shrugged, holding his palms up apologetically.

Cyello belted back his tankard and stood—allowing Korwynn and Tiny room to slide free of the bench—his vigilant eyes taking in the people at the tables around them.

A vision of Allard and the couple whose window she had destroyed screamed at her. In desperate need of assistance, they needed help now. Their plight couldn't wait for the baron's restructuring plans of Storms End to take effect. They'd be long dead by then.

Korwynn slid to the end of the bench and attempted to stand but Larina slapped his wrist hard—holding it against the table.

Korwynn jerked to a halt.

Bear tensed beside her.

"I'll do it," she whispered so quietly, she wasn't sure she had spoken out loud.

"What's that?" Korwynn growled.

"I'll do it."

Korwynn snatched his hand free—his chin firm as he glared death at her. "The price is three hundred, now."

Larina stood, rage flaring her nostrils. If not for Bear's steadying hand on her forearm, she wasn't sure what she would have done. She was vaguely aware of the hush that had settled over the tavern. Through gritted teeth, she replied, "Three fifty."

"I'm sorry? Did you say, two fifty?"

She wanted to scream. Contemplating pulling her dagger and burying it into the beast of a man, she swallowed and said with venom, "Three hundred."

Korwynn straightened to his full six-foot-six height. Stretching his thick neck, he nodded to Tiny to move back onto the bench.

Once seated, Tiny threw a worn leather purse across the table.

Lithe as a cat, Larina snatched the bag out of the air; its contents jingling. She didn't dare count it at the table.

"Perfect. Cyello, provide our new partner with the specifics of what she needs to know. By this time, three days hence, Miss Bolt will be a rich woman." Korwynn caught the barmaid's attention before locking eyes with Larina. "Be prepared to stay here all night if you wish to have any chance of surviving a foray into one of the most heavily guarded homesteads outside of Castle Svelte."

Larina

Affairs in Order

Brilliant sunshine blinded Larina's bloodshot eyes as she exited the *Kraken's Curse* the next morning. She had remained awake through the night, learning in detail about the nuances of the job Korwynn and his cohorts had hired her to undertake.

Good old Bear had remained with her throughout it all, ordering her food and generally watching over her—his presence calming her whenever something her employers said rattled her senses. He had even tended to her hurts as best as he could.

Rock had joined them for a while as discussions became heated regarding how she was to go about executing the acquisition of the scroll. The Rock's company allowed her to become bolder than she might have on her own. In the end, Korwynn and his lackeys had left her and Bear shortly after the sun pushed aside the darkness.

Stretching her stiff muscles, she waved a dismissive hand at Bear's waddling bulk as he rounded the front corner of the *Kraken's Curse* and disappeared to wherever he spent his days. There was something not quite right with her old friend, but she couldn't put a name to it. Perhaps she would ask him when they met again in two night's time.

She smiled as she thought of Bear. At one point, she had known everything about him, but as the years passed and she became more embroiled in the underground of Storms End, she had, out of necessity, stopped volunteering information about herself to anyone. Nor did she wish to know anything about those Bear hung around on the occasions their paths crossed. The less she knew, the less chance someone would seek her out to squeeze information from.

Few people knew her real name. Two in fact. Bear and Rock. The former would die before he gave it away and the latter would kill anyone who asked. As for a surname, she never knew her sire so she had never cared. Her mother had called her Larina, and the people living in the streets were her family. That was good enough for her.

She caressed the bulging sack of coins hidden beneath her tunic. If she had any money left after seeing to the others, a good fitting set of warmer clothes would be in order.

She wiped at bits of sleep in the corners of her eyes. It was time to put her good fortune to work. She was in serious need of a proper rest, but first, she had to check on the welfare of an old friend.

Cold fear tingled her spine as she prodded the pile of burlap sacks with her boot. A solid object beneath the tattered cloth resisted her touch.

Uncaring about the curious stares her actions elicited from passers by in the street, she dropped a wooden bucket she had filled with all sorts of food she had purchased in the lower market. Its contents tumbled onto the dirt encrusted cobblestones. Discarding a pile of cloth draped over her forearm, she crouched and ripped the sacks off the unmoving body of Allard.

Tears welling up, she stretched out a shaking hand and touched his wrinkled neck. The cold, chicken-like skin beneath her fingers made her gasp. Crouching in the alley with a bag full of coin at her belt, she was too late to save her friend. She covered her face and wept.

A skeleton-like hand reached out to grab her elbow. “You know I can’t stand it to see you cry, lassie.”

The burlap sacks spilled about Allard’s form as he stiffly rose to a sitting position.

Sure her heart skipped a beat, she dropped to her knees and grasped his bony shoulders. The reek of sweat and bad breath turned up her nostrils, but she didn’t care. “You’re alive?”

“Of course, I’m alive. Take more ‘n a few runts high on their own worth to take down brave, old, Sir Allard.”

She snorted a wet laugh and leaned into him; hugging him as tightly as she dared. “I should never doubt you.”

She felt his stick frame swell with pride in her grasp. She cried harder.

“Here, here, lassie. Allard’s got ya. Ain’t nobody gonna hurt you while I draw air.”

His words raised a suffocating lump in her throat. She squeezed tighter. Matted with filth, his long, wiry hair, itched her face and neck but she didn’t care. She whispered into his ear, “I know. Thank you. And I won’t let anything happen to you, either. I promise.”

Wiping her cheeks on her shoulders, she leaned back and smiled into Allard’s kind eyes. “I’ve brought you something.”

“Och lass. I don’t think I can handle a young one at my age.”

She laughed and shook her head. Always the jokester. As bleak as his future was, he never once complained. Over the few years that she’d known him, Allard had become her sounding board whenever she despaired. She swallowed at the absurdity of life. Here she was in her prime, spry and able to make a living, as nefarious as her choices were becoming, and yet she drew strength from a man whose life had passed him by and could no longer look after himself.

She collected the contents of her bucket and cleared a space to sit beside him.

She passed him a skinny loaf of bread wrapped in cloth. "Here."

They ate in silence; a beggar's feast of juicy fruits, bread, and cheese—washing it down with watery wine and enjoying the warmth of the sun as it passed above the alleyway.

Larina brushed the crumbs from her lap and stood. Peering down the street to where the bay lay far below, she sighed. Storm clouds were forming over the snowy peaks on the horizon.

"Come on. I've found a new place for you to rest your weary bones."

His gapped-tooth smirk prepared her for his reply.

"I'm flattered, but an old-fashioned man, such as myself, must insist we're properly married."

A sadness crept through her as she smiled for his benefit. He was such an endearing man. He would have made someone a happy woman in his time. She chastised herself. He could still make a woman happy.

She nodded, her forced smile softening into a sly grin.

He tilted his head. "What's so funny? You don't think you can handle me?"

"Hah! Oh, I'm sure I could, but I've got something better in mind."

He raised bushy, unkempt eyebrows. "Do tell."

"If you wanna find out, you'll have to follow me." She winked.

"Like that, is it?" He held a shaky hand out to her. "Well, come on. You can't expect me to do everything, can you? Give an old fella a hand."

She checked the street one last time to ensure she didn't see anyone who might be looking for her. Satisfied, she grasped the handle of the bucket with one hand and gently hoisted Allard to his feet with the other—hanging onto him until he steadied himself.

"You okay?"

"Bah. Ain't never been better. If I wasn't afraid of breaking your confidence, I'd show you how a king's soldier marches."

"Thank you. That's very kind." She patted his hand and grabbed him by the elbow. "Why don't you escort me, then?"

He nodded and did his best to straighten his stooped form. With Larina on his arm, he ambled from the alley and tried to turn left.

Larina gently urged him the other way. "This way, oh noble knight."

Allard made an indignant snort and lifted his chin high. "Of course it's this way."

The sun on her face, and hanging onto Allard's arm, Larina found her cheeks bursting with joy. Rare were the days she actually loved life. For all of the hardships she and everyone she assisted endured, moments like this made everything worthwhile. Not even the brooding clouds parading down Thunderhead Fjord could dampen her spirits. Seeing the proud face of one of Zephyr's grizzled warriors was like viewing the rainbow before the storm.

"And just where is Miss Bolt leading me?"

She squeezed his forearm. "Oh, you'll see. A palace befitting a royal knight."

Allard's posture straightened a bit more.

"Here we are, Sir Allard."

Two tiers below the alley where Allard had rested after being evicted from the last building he had squatted in, they stood arm-in-arm, gazing at the crumbling façade of a leaning stone and wood structure; three stories high. Black smears around window wells, and charred balcony walls, gave evidence to the fire that had ravaged the building during Helleden Misenthorpe's foray into Zephyr.

Observing it in the daylight, Larina wasn't sure she had made a good choice in bringing Allard here.

The look on his face spoke otherwise. "That's a right regal sight for aged eyes, lass. A proper bastion for a knight of the realm."

She swallowed the thickening lump of despair in her throat and muttered, "Aged eyes for sure."

In his youth, Allard the knight would have towered over Larina's taller than average height, but time had taken its toll. He looked up at her. "Eh?"

She didn't bother repeating herself. "I agree. A fortress befitting Zephyr's finest warrior."

She released him. The bucket of food and clothing in one hand, she pointed her free arm at the missing front doors. "Your castle awaits."

Holding his head high, he threw back his shoulders as best as he was able and high-stepped across the threshold—careful not to step in a puddle of what Larina suspected to be urine just inside.

A ravaged foyer of charred timber and cracked stone circled the remains of a large fountain. On either side of the dusty, debris-filled space, staircases stripped of whatever had covered them once upon a time, curved their way to a dark landing above—the left staircase missing its last several steps.

Guilt plagued Larina as she examined the structure. “Perhaps this isn’t the place I thought it was.”

Allard’s intense stare scrutinized the foyer as he slowly shuffled in a circle. When his grey eyes met hers, he smiled. “It’s perfect.”

Without waiting, he shuffled to the right staircase and grabbed its wobbly rail. “Are you coming, my princess?”

Larina swallowed her misgivings. Fighting back tears she didn’t understand, she put on a brave face and caught up to him before he reached the third step. She took his arm and gently helped lift his insignificant weight up the remaining stairs.

The landing overlooking the foyer below was framed with jagged pieces of what once must have been a grand balustrade. Several rooms led off the landing on three sides. A few of the doorways were covered with dangling rags or discoloured sheets but for the most part, the blackened rooms visible in the muted light filtering through open windows and yellowed glass were cluttered with fallen walls and broken rafters.

A single staircase wound its way up from the centre of the platform to the level above. The same stairwell the man and the mysterious archer had come at her from.

If Allard was reconsidering her choice of accommodations, his face didn’t reflect it. His old eyes surveyed the landing like they had caught sight of a long-lost lover. Larina imagined the old knight had known this building in all of its former grandeur in his earlier years.

Larina

More to keep her own mind from imagining the horrors that had filled the once grand building during the sorcerer's attack on the bay area, she said, "I want you to meet some new friends of mine. I dropped in on them unexpectedly last night."

"Lead on, Princess Bolt." He held out an arm and they ascended the wide steps together.

Upon reaching the next level, Larina looked down and caught her breath. In her mind's eye she saw the city Watchman and the female archer charging after her. She reeled momentarily; the weight of the bucket dragged at her.

Allard pulled on her arm. "Easy, lass. You'd not want to fall back down."

She swallowed. "No. No I wouldn't." Recovering, she led him to the gaping doorway on their right.

As soon as she reached the threshold, she knew something was wrong. An odour she had smelled too many times before opened her eyes wide. She released Allard and ran into the room, shaking her head as she went. The word, 'no' repeated itself in her mind; over and over and over again. The forgotten bucket of food clattered on the floor, spilling its contents.

Entangled in sticklike arms, the elderly couple stared vacantly at each other as if about to share an intimate kiss—their ashen skin an unnatural shade.

Green eyes looked up from the man's lap—the mangy-furred, brown cat she had startled last night watched her approach. Before she got close, it scrambled to its feet and disappeared through the window she had broken.

The cat's departure exposed the couples' blood-stained clothing near their waist. Someone had impaled them with a sword.

Larina

"No, no, no, no." Larina dropped to her knees. "Please, no."

Though her brain told her they were long dead, her heart refused to believe. Barely able to draw breath, she felt their necks.

Footsteps shuffled up from behind. The compassion in Allard's voice sent shivers through her. "They're gone, lassie. There's nothing you could have done."

Her body violently trembling from head to foot, she craned her tear-streaked face to him. "You don't understand. It's my fault. I led the butchers to them…" Her voice dropped away and she dropped to her backside, holding her hands over her face. "I killed them, Allard. I killed them."

"Are you sure you'll be okay here?" Larina stared out the multi-paned window at the sun setting over the fjord. Black clouds wisped across its face, promising an unsettled evening.

Dressed in baggy, new clothes and sitting beside a fur-lined, leather surcoat she had purchased for him, the colour in Allard's face showed a much healthier hue.

His beaming face helped her forget the crushing guilt of the old couple. "Living the life of good King Malcolm, I am."

Distracted, she smiled half-heartedly. It was time she paid back the evil the Watch had perpetrated.

Her thoughts drifted to the old couple. Their bodies lay in an abandoned wine cellar beneath the basement. It would be best to get them out of there soon and interred, but she couldn't do it on her own. She required the help of Bear and his associates.

"Huh? Oh, yes." She knelt beside him and pulled a long surcoat, emblazoned with a coat-of-arms she wasn't familiar with, from the pile of clothes beside him and draped it over his lap. "You make a fine king. I would bend my knee to you any day."

"Och lassie. You're daft in the head. I'm a fighting man through and through. I ain't cut out for the lavish court life."

She unfolded a thin blanket and draped it around his shoulders. "There. That should keep you warm."

Thunder rumbled in the distance.

"Make sure you keep away from the window. By the look of the floorboards, I'm thinking the window leaks."

Allard twitched his head, trying to prevent her ministrations. "Stuff your fussing. You're worse than my blessed mother; may the gods keep her safe 'til I see her again."

Something in his words struck a chord in her. She froze and gazed into his cheerful eyes. For some intangible reason, she knew she'd never see him again.

She sucked in a deep breath and bit on her lower lip—doing her best to keep it from quivering. Shoring up her mental fortitude, she kept his stare. "I may not be back for a while."

Allard tilted his head. "Leaving me for a younger knight, are ya?"

She frowned, not expecting that. Catching his slight smile, she shook her head and laughed. "All the king's horses couldn't pull me away. You know that."

He patted her knee. "I'm just playing with you, my sweet friend. Allard would never keep you from your true heart's desire."

"It's not that. Trust me. Nothing could be farther from the truth. I'm happy being single." She stared vacantly at the darkening windowpanes. “If I’m not mistaken, I always will be. It would take a very, *very* special man to take your place.”

She pulled a few wisps of his straggly hair from the corners of his face; absently making a promise to herself that when she returned, she’d give him a nice shave. He always liked a clean face.

“No, I have business to attend to.”

Skeletal fingers dug into her thigh. “Is it dangerous?”

She dipped her head with a shrug. “Aye. It may be. But not to worry. Nothing can stop a lightning bolt.”

He held her stare—a strength she had never seen before shone behind his eyes.

She tried to stand and put space between them but with surprisingly quick reflexes, he clasped her hands in his bony clutches and held her fast.

“You must do what you need to do. I can see by the look in your pretty eyes that you’re about to do something you feel strongly about. Whatever it is, make sure you do it well.”

His grip was incredible—to the point that she wanted to cry out, but she refused to show weakness in his presence. “I will. If I succeed, well…let’s just say, life for you, and many others, is going to change for the better. You’ll see.”

His grey eyes hardened—their intensity scaring her.

“Larina…”

She gaped. How did he know her name?

“…aye. I know who you are.”

Her eyes grew wide with speculation. Could he be…?

“Listen to me. I’m not long for this world.”

“Don’t say that.”

“Do not fear for me. I look forward to being reunited with my real princess. She’s waited a long time.”

Tears rolled down her cheeks. “No. Tell her she has to wait longer.”

Larina

"Larina. Hear me." His voice was deep and authoritative. "Life isn't a dress rehearsal. You don't get to come back and do it all over again. You must grasp life and live it the way that makes *you* happy. Don't let others choose your path. Reach out with everything you have and grasp your dream."

She nodded, trying to hold his stare through tear-blurred vision.

"Life's a convoluted journey. Not a race. Slow down and live *your* life. Not mine. Not the couple enjoying the comforts of the wine cellar. *Your* life. You understand what I'm saying?"

She nodded even though she really didn't.

"You must forget about us and get your own affairs in order. We appreciate and love you for all you do, but it's time you lived *your* life. Whether you're highborn or just some drunk in an ill-begotten seaport, in the end, the destination is the same for each and every one of us." He nodded at her wondering gaze. "Aye. A casket."

Larina

Their Own Kind of Compassion

Lightning illuminated the lone watchtower on the northwest edge of Storms End. Slick with rain, ominous black stone refracted the bright flash of jagged energy arcing over the churning waters of Thunderhead Fjord.

Drenched to the skin, her back against the wall of rock towering overhead and out of sight, Larina shivered profusely. She didn't care. Her mind was focused on her surroundings.

Catlike instincts and uncanny perception allowed her to slink about the shadows with little fear of attracting attention. Years of stealthy manoeuvring to obtain the bare necessities of life had instilled in her an unnatural ability to climb, slip through, unlock, and unearth things that most people couldn't comprehend were at play around them.

The vision of the elderly couple refused to leave her thoughts. She feared she might do something careless as a result, but her deeper dread of Allard's deteriorating condition drove her on. It was time for the hunted Storms End Lightning Bolt to become Larina the hunter. A transition that suited her unique talents well.

Driving rain stuck her long, brown hair to her face like a cowl. Her exposed face dripped with black soot—a camouflage she employed when skulking about after sundown. Clad in dark leather from head to toe, her black gloved hand habitually ensured the dagger at her waist remained firmly seated within its sheath.

Under cover of a long rumble of thunder, she padded from one shadow to the next. The hunter closed in on her unwitting prey.

She ducked beneath a low overhang of natural rock jutting out from the fjord wall; several paces from the solitary entrance to the watchtower. Craning her neck, the yellowish glow at the top of the narrow tower shone dimly; warning boats of danger. Across the bay, a similar light could just be seen through the downpour.

As she suspected, nobody was out tonight. The dropping temperatures and driving storm kept even the hardiest of guards within their shelters, but she wasn't a fool. Though not visible, they would be around somewhere.

A smug grin tightened her lips. No matter where they were, they would never suspect the Lightning Bolt striking from a vantage point only a bird or a hardy troll would dare attempt.

In rapid succession, three forks of lightning jagged above different sections of Storms End, casting the skyline in an eerie silhouette. Larina took advantage of the brilliant flashes to reconnoitre the base of the tower. A halberd glinted in the lightning flashes, exposing a lone guard braving the elements.

As easy as it would be to sneak up behind the guard by slinking along the rock-strewn shoreline and over the butte of rock at the tower's base, Larina wasn't interested in killing just anyone. Her prey was too high and mighty to be caught out on a miserable night like tonight. No, Danth Emerald, one of the captains of the Storms End Watch, would be lounging before a blazing fire, planning new ways to make the lives of the less fortunate a continuing nightmare.

Larina

Waiting on the next lightning flash to confirm the guard hadn't moved, Larina slipped through the cascade of water running off the edge of the overhang and darted into the shadows beyond the doorway.

A deep cough made her freeze. She grasped the hilt of her dagger and looked over her shoulder, but nothing moved in the downpour.

Several quick steps and she was behind the tower's curving wall. Taking a moment to catch her breath and still her hammering heart, she clenched her wet gloves a few times as she surveyed the near vertical climb. In good conditions, scaling the tower would have tested her skills, but in the incessant rain, it struck her as a fool's errand. She doubted a troll would hazard the wall tonight.

She firmed her resolve. It might be some time before an opportunity like this presented itself again. Getting out of the tower afterward might prove problematic, but she didn't care. Danth would be lying in his own blood, along with anyone else foolish enough to confront her. It was time to treat these people with their own kind of compassion.

Flexing her fingers, she located a small depression between two large wall stones and began her ascent toward a black slot midway up the tower's lofty height. The slot would likely open onto a stairwell. Her only fear was once she attained the opening, it wouldn't be wide enough to slip her skinny body through.

Scouting the tower from various vantage points over the last few weeks, she had entertained just such a scenario, but had never been brazen enough to attempt the manoeuvre. The couple's murder had changed all that. Rather, Danth Emerald's increased brutality had made the decision for her. It was only a matter of time before he ordered the execution of everyone squatting in the upper tiers. That meant Allard too, and *that*, Larina would not stand for.

The climb, slipperier in the rain, was taxing on her arms and fingers. Her supple boots clung to faint nuances in the stone's seams, allowing her to rest, spread-eagled on the side of the tower like a four-legged spider frozen for the winter.

Craning her neck, she couldn't see her objective, but she knew it was there. She just had to get to it. Thankful little wind accompanied the storm, she pushed everything from her mind. With practised concentration, her only goal was to achieve the next layer of rock. And then the next. And the next. One arm up high, followed by the opposite leg. One imperfection in the wall's surface after another.

The rain eased and the swirling mass of dark clouds broke. The dark watchtower glistened in the ensuing moonlight, its bulk standing silent vigil over the bay. Larina clung to the wall, halfway to its summit, a curious dark blotch exposed to anyone who might cast an eye her way.

Her thighs screamed and her fingers ached so bad she wanted to cry, but there was nothing to do but fall to her death or climb higher.

A gasp of relevance escaped her bluish lips. The window slot met her probing upper hand—shocking her to the point that she nearly slipped from the wall. Swallowing her near brush with death, she concentrated on locating her next foothold. Her opposite arm lifted higher than her first; allowing her to wrap her forearm over the ledge.

She froze. A fleeting dread tensed her muscles. What if someone chose to climb the stairwell at that moment? She shook the thought away. The longer she lingered, the greater chance that might happen. She had to get through the window as quickly as possible.

Shoring up her next toehold, she hoisted and pulled until her head breached the opening. Heaving heavy breaths, panic seized her. The slot was too narrow for her shoulders. Looking down, something she had trained herself not to do, the ground seemed to swirl around the tower's base. There was no way she could ease her way back down. She lacked the strength.

One deep breath. Two deep breaths. Finding another precarious toe hold a little higher up, she lifted her shoulders over the stone window sill and twisted her body sideways as she grabbed hold of the inside of the thick window opening and pulled herself through until her weight rested on her ribs.

Had she not been so terrified, she would have laughed as she envisioned what she must look like to a casual observer. She was grateful for the cover of darkness and the ever-present threat of trolls at night. Anyone still awake would prefer to remain within the taverns or beneath a candle at home. Fortunately, the window she hung suspended in faced down the fjord, away from Storms End.

She drew several deep, calming breaths and turned her head to squeeze it all the way through.

Her breath caught in her throat.

She had been right about where the window had been built. Visible in the scant light offered by sporadic sconces set randomly along walls, a steep flight of wooden stairs spiralled up and down the inside of the tower—on the opposite side from where she struggled. She swallowed and twisted as much as she could in order to see the wall below where she lay. To her horror, it fell away for twenty or more feet before the stairwell passed beneath her position. Looking up, she could just make out the underside of the steps; their treads held against the wall by supports embedded in the stone blocks. The distance to reach them was at least twice her height.

The inside slope of the tower walls filled her with a paralyzing realization that there was no way she could possibly cling to them. Nor did she wish to entertain trying to wriggle her body back out and climb down the tower's exterior. Staring at the opposing stairwell, she was left with two choices. Exit the tower with the hope of making it to the top before her strength gave out, *or*, jump across the inside gap and hope to land on the narrow steps without falling into the gaping hollow in the tower's centre and embracing a quick death.

She clenched her hands; aching fingers answering the question for her. Now all she had to do was figure out how to manipulate her body in the tight confines of the window enclosure to permit her a chance to make the attempt.

A random bang somewhere within the tower made her stare wide-eyed into the darkness below but no sound accompanied the noise. Daring to breathe again, she lifted her body sideways in the opening—carefully manoeuvring her shoulders beyond the edge of the inside wall. If not for the firm hold her thighs maintained on the sides of the window well, she would have pitched forward.

The jump facing her was no bigger than one of the wider jumps across the narrow streets she entertained while roof hopping, but this time she was stationary. The gap would have to be spanned by the power in her legs alone. There would be no residual momentum assisting this leap.

Taking a deep breath, she prepared mentally, feeling the window's edges slipping under the pressure she exerted to keep from falling. A quick intake of breath and a sudden bend in her knees precipitated the jump, just as a hollow thud echoed inside the stairwell and light flooded into the chamber far below.

Startled, she teetered and almost fell. At the last moment, she sprang across the gap; arms flailing and legs running through the air.

She hit the opposite wall harder than anticipated. The impact of her landing and the scrape of her dagger's handle off the far wall thundered in the enclosed space. It was all she could do not to fall backward over the edge of the shaking stairwell as she crouched and unsuccessfully tried to hold her breath. For a moment, she feared the wooden structure would collapse beneath her.

"Oi! Who's up there?" A male's voice sounded hollowly from below. "Is that you, Danth?"

Larina swallowed, casting a wild gaze around in the semi-darkness. The flickering radiance below was moving around the perimeter of the tower, its glow climbing the wall.

Quiet as a cat, she padded up the steps as fast as her tired legs would carry her. Adrenaline got her to the top faster than she thought possible, to where a plain, wooden door blocked her progress. Thankfully, a quick push on its latch was all it took for it to creak open.

A blast of heat hit her full in the face from a large firepit set into the middle of the square, glass-framed room. Chopped wood sat in a long pile along the landward side of the chamber; leaving the fjord-facing windows clear.

Whoever climbed after her didn't appear to be in a hurry. She eased the door shut, cringing as its squeal caterwauled in the stairwell.

"Captain?" the voice asked. "Is that—"

The door latched shut, cutting off his voice.

Larina studied the beacon room. There was no place to hide. Her dagger leapt into her hand as her heart jumped into her throat. She had come here seeking to kill the Captain of the Watch, Danth Emerald. Because of the pain and death the captain had perpetrated, she had no qualms about ending his life, but the person climbing the steps wasn't Danth.

Once whoever it was realized she didn't belong there, she would be forced to kill him or be taken into custody. After everything she had done over the last few years, to be caught by the Storms End Watch meant certain death.

She doubted they'd allow her to leave the tower alive, so she resigned herself to the task at hand.

Larina

Signal Fire

Creaking wood and the squeal of rusty hinges announced the leery entrance of the man climbing the stairwell of the northwest watchtower. A handheld sconce tentatively entered the beacon room on the end of an arm. "Danth?"

Hiding behind the door, Larina clutched a thick chunk of firewood; waiting for the right moment to club the man in the head with the hope of knocking him unconscious so she wouldn't have to kill him.

Everything happened so fast. One moment, she was holding her breath in the deathly silent chamber—the crackling and snapping of the signal fire and her heavy breathing all that disturbed the silence high above Storms End. Though the heat in the room was insufferable, she had no choice but to put up with it as she waited. The next moment, the man peered around the leading edge of the door and locked eyes with her.

She pulled the door wide open and swung out with the small log, but he stepped back against the pile of stacked wood. Her errant strike smashed the oil-filled sconce from his hand; shattering it on the floor between them. Oil spilled and ignited, flowing across the floor and under the wood pile. She dropped the chunk in her hand in shock, and pulled her dagger free; watching in horror as the realization of what had just happened sunk in.

Larina

"It's you!" The man pointed a short sword at her but struggled to keep his attention on her backing around the fjord side of the chamber—his gaze kept jumping to the new fire in the room. "Look what you've done!"

He stepped away from the catching wood pile, clearly in the throes of indecision as to whether he should go after her or try to quench the building flames. "Drop your weapon or I'll be forced to use my sword."

She studied his face. Though she didn't personally know him, she knew him as Fren. One of the Watch who had hounded her many times in the past—never quite being able to get his hands on her. Standing between her and the door with a sword in hand, it seemed now would be his chance.

Larina, the hunter, had other ideas. She sidestepped, keeping as much distance between them as possible. She doubted he would be so foolish as to jump across the large signal fire. "Drop your sword, and I'll let you live."

Even in her own mind, the threat sounded preposterous. Fren was a member of the Watch—a hired thug who dealt with unruly and lawbreaking members of society on a daily basis. How did a young woman, armed with a dagger, expect to dispatch one such as he?

Her threat gave Fren pause. His gaze jumped back and forth between the fire climbing the wall and her as she kept bobbing back and forth on the balls of her feet.

The heat of the new fire drove him past the door—a smug smile turning up his lips. "You've got nowhere to go. Let's see the Lightning Bolt zap her way out of this." He sidestepped; his sword at the ready—shepherding her around the exterior of the small room toward the increasing conflagration that was quickly getting out of control.

Larina

Sweat dripped down her face, absorbing into her wet, leather clothing. If they didn't get out of the room soon, neither one of them would live to see the sunrise.

A large chunk of wood in the signal fire attracted her attention. Mostly engulfed in fire and covered in patches of red-hot embers, an unburnt edge faced her. "Last warning, Fren. It doesn't have to end this way."

The fact that she mentioned him by name, visibly threw him. He frowned. "Pfft. Or what?"

"Or this." She moved so quickly, Fren froze, unable to do anything but jump back toward the door as she grabbed hold of the burning chunk of wood and threw it at him—purposely dropping it between them in a flurry of sparks and splintering wood.

"Nice." He laughed; his attention drawn by the errant piece of burning wood. "What's that supposed to…? Hey!"

Larina took advantage of his momentary lapse of concentration and sprinted toward the fire engulfing the stacked wood. She leaped and landed on top of the pile, ducking to keep from hitting her head off the blackening rafters.

The pile shifted under her feet; collapsing toward the middle of the room and the open doorway. Several burning logs tumbled across the threshold and disappeared into the blackness beyond.

She landed before the doorway, barely able to keep her feet under her—surprise written on her face.

Fren came at her. Keeping his sword between them, he approached the threshold and stopped to peer down. "What have you done?"

Larina stepped back, wary of his sword's tip.

"If that catches the stairwell," Fren spun on her, a maniacal glint in his eyes, "we'll both fry."

Larina

"Then I suggest you let me go."

"Let you go?" Fren gaped. "After everything you've done? The captain would flay me alive."

She shrugged, raising her eyebrows. "Who says he has to know?"

Fren couldn't stop staring down the shaft. He noticeably swallowed. Wavering his sword, he took a tentative step toward her. "Drop the dagger or I'll run you through." He hazarded a concerned look at the open doorway.

She ignored his threat. "Where's Danth?"

Fren's face scrunched up in question. "He's not here."

"Liar. I saw him enter the tower at nightfall."

Fren took a hesitant step toward her. "Well he ain't here now."

"What? Where'd he go?"

"How would I know? He went to check on something."

The growing flames at Larina's back barred any chance of her escaping Fren's sword.

A small log rolled free of the burning pile she had dislodged and bumped against her ankle. She hooked it with the toe of her boot and kicked out, flinging the burning chunk through the air.

Fren cried out, lifting his arms to keep the offending brand from taking him in the face.

She wasted no time charging in behind. Lifting a leg high, she extended it and drove the bottom of her foot into Fren's chest; slamming him into the glass wall on the far side of the door.

Not waiting to see if her kick had incapacitated him, Larina dashed through the door and scrambled down the rickety stairwell—her hurried footsteps shaking the structure as her right hand slid along the interior wall for support. Far below, a growing orange glow confirmed Fren's fear. The stairwell had caught fire.

"Stop!" Fren called after her.

She felt his footfalls on the stairwell but didn't dare look back. She couldn't stop her headlong descent if she wanted to.

"You crazy woman! Look what you've done! Halt!"

A window slot passed by on the opposite wall. She had no way of knowing but she was certain it was the one she had climbed through. If that was true, she had a long way to go before she reached the bottom.

Smoke billowed up the shaft, making visibility difficult. If not for her leading hand sliding along the wall, she would have run off the narrow steps.

The heat in the stairwell increased considerably. Within the growing flames she thought she saw a door open at the base of the stairs.

A female voice called out. "Fren! What have you done?"

Flames lapped at the edges of the steps beneath Larina's feet as she approached the ground.

"Stop her! It's the Lightning Bolt!" Fren shouted from somewhere above.

Larina rounded the interior of the wall until the open doorway lay in sight; still a decent drop away.

Clad in Watch livery, a woman squinted up at her, her eyes growing wide as she realized who was barreling down on her. She grasped her sword hilt and started to pull it free but let it go and crossed her forearms above her head as the Storms End Lightning Bolt jumped from the stairwell.

Larina used the woman to break her fall; driving her to the ground. They fell through the open door into a small room beyond—the impact knocking the woman senseless. Larina raised her dagger, prepared to strike, but held back. The woman wasn't the archer who had chased her the other night.

Taking a quick look at the stairwell door, Larina half-expected to see Fren charge through, but only flames greeted her gaze. She got to her feet, located a door on the opposite side of the room, and bolted from the chamber.

The door led to a flight of stone steps with a large, open room at its base. She didn't bother to inspect the map laid out on a large table in the middle of the chamber. If she didn't get out of the watchtower at once, she'd have to face the entire city guard. Visions of how the out of control fire high atop the tower must appear from outside urged her to move faster.

A cold gust of night air slammed into her as she opened the exterior door and surprised a lone guard huddled underneath the protruding lintel stone—the man totally unaware of what was happening.

He jumped to his feet, grasping his polearm in both hands. "Who are—"

She grabbed him by the arm and yanked him backward into the open air. "No time to explain. Hurry. The tower's burning!"

The man's face turned ashen.

Larina impelled him toward the door. "Hurry. They need you."

His polearm clattered off the natural stone surrounding the entrance to the tower as he disappeared inside.

Running as fast as she could along the narrow strip of navigable land connecting the watchtower to Storms End, her jaw dropped. Despite her urgency to flee, she staggered to a halt. The outer walls of the lofty watchtower were surrounded by roiling black smoke. Flames licked at random stairwell window slots. The entire structure reflected eerily on the black water of the fjord and the rain soaked cliffside behind it. The sight took her breath away.

A loud crash echoed all over the bay area as the intense heat blew out the massive wall of windows high atop the beacon tower.

Awed by the amount of damage her foray had created, a cocky grin split her lips. Judging by how high the flames leaped into the air from the tower's summit, she mused that the signal fire might be visible all the way to Thunderhead.

Larina

Conflicting Emotions

Bear gaped incredulously. "That was you?"

Larina nodded, embarrassed.

The big man scanned the tavern as if searching for trouble. He returned an open-mouthed stare her way; shoving his massive bulk against her—squishing her into the wall and blocking anyone's view.

A meaty arm wrapped around her head, pulling her into his side. "You'll have everyone in the Watch searching for you. We need to hide you."

She used her hands to pry her head free of his embrace. Shaking out her hair, she glared at him. "You trying to kill me?"

"Trying to save your pretty arse, more like."

"Snapping my head off isn't the best way to save me."

He put a sausage-sized finger to his lips. "Hush, lassie. Not even Rock can keep Danth and his goons from the *Curse* for long. We need to get you outta here."

"And just where do you propose I go? They'll be…" She trailed off; her eyes wild. "No!"

She placed a foot on the bench and attempted to leap over the table.

Bear latched onto her shoulders and forced her back down. "Where are you going?"

"I gotta get back to Allard and the others. The Watch will kill them."

Larina

"And what can you do to stop them?" Bear growled, struggling to hold her in place despite his superior strength. "Nothing, that's what."

"Let go! I can't just let them die." She studied his corded forearm and considered biting him.

He tightened his grip and shook her. "You don't know that. Calm down. You're drawing attention to yourself."

The usual cacophony of the *Kraken's Curse* had dropped to a dull ebb. Everyone looked at the table along the back wall where a goliath of a man and a young woman argued.

Larina stopped struggling, her eyes searching the room for people she didn't recognize as regulars. There were always a few who came in with the tide, but no one appeared to be overly interested in the commotion she and Bear were making.

Seeing that the domestic dispute had run its course, the patrons lost interest and returned to their own affairs.

Bear glowered at a few lollygaggers until they looked away. He plopped his bear paws over Larina's hands and looked her in the eye. "Now tell me. What happened?"

"With the tower?"

Bear rolled his eyes.

Larina swallowed, feeling colour rush to her cheeks. "It's a long story."

"Aye, I bet. Always is with you."

She leaned in close and lowered her voice; scanning the barroom. "You remember the elderly couple I mentioned to you after Korwynn and his men left?"

His eyes searched the rafters as if seeking the answer. He nodded as it came to him. "Yes. The ones you dropped in on while Danth and that mysterious archer woman chased you. What of them?"

Her breath quickened. "That bastard killed them."

Larina

Bear's head continued to bob at her words. "And so, you torched the watchtower?"

"No...! Well...Yes. Sort of." She looked sheepishly into his warm eyes. "I didn't mean to. It just...sort of happened."

He grunted. "Sort of happened? You just, *sort* of burned one of the Watch's main towers? Accidentally, of course."

"Yes." She smiled at his disbelieving face. "I'm serious. I didn't plan to set a stone tower on fire. I'm not crazy."

He raised his eyebrows as if he wasn't convinced.

She lowered her voice to a whisper. "I went there with the intention of killing Danth Emerald. Things got a little out of hand."

"A little, huh?" He shook his head. "Honestly, Bolt. How have you managed to stay alive this long?"

She smiled and hugged his bicep, placing her face against his reassuring mass. "I don't know. Just lucky, I guess."

"Seems to me your luck's running out."

She leaned her head back to lock stares. "Why's that? It's just a tower. They'll rebuild it in no time."

"But now you'll have the Watch after you."

"Like that's something new."

"I'm serious, Bolt. Danth may have had a bone to pick with you before, but when the baron hears of this, he'll spare no expense to see you in irons." He hung his head and mumbled. "Or worse."

Larina studied Bear's sad face, allowing the bar sounds to wash over her. Though her leather clothing was still damp, the cozy warmth of the tavern was comforting.

She hugged his arm tighter. "Aw. You really do care about me."

He cleared his throat and patted her head with a free hand. "Of course, I do. And, I'm afraid for you. Mark my words. If you don't stop travelling the dark paths you've chosen lately, you'll end up in the ground like the couple you spoke of."

This wasn't the first time he'd expressed this point of view. Although she loved him for it, his words bounced off her like rain from her tunic.

"Speaking of the old couple, I have a favour to ask. I dragged their bodies to the wine cellar to keep them from smelling, but I can't get them to the top of the fjord to bury them."

He nodded. "Let me know where and I'll have my mates retrieve them."

"You're a real chum."

"It'll cost ya."

She patted the money pouch hidden beneath her tunic and winked as the coins chinked. "I'm good for it."

He leaned back, shrugging his arm free. "Speaking of which, I wanted to talk to you about your arrangement with Korwynn."

She took a healthy swig from her neglected tankard. "What of it?"

"I want you to reconsider."

"Reconsider? You're the one who set us up."

"I did, but that was before I knew what they had in mind."

"You didn't object when you found out. Why now?"

"I didn't object because I was worried about how they'd react."

She blinked several times, trying to come to terms with his admission. "*You*? Afraid of someone?"

He raised his eyebrows. "Ya, well, let's just say these men don't strike me as everyday criminals."

"Why's that?"

"They have access to great amounts of coin, for starters."

"So?"

Larina

"Doesn't it strike you as strange that they already have lots of coin at their disposal, and yet, are willing to part with it to acquire a simple scroll?"

She tilted her head and shrugged. "Makes no difference to me. I've learned not to ask too many questions. If they're willing to pay good coin, I'm in."

He ran his hand through his beard. "I don't like it."

She raised her eyebrows for him to elaborate.

"I know the Banebridges. Well, I know Thoril's son. I chummed with him before he went east to enlist with the King's Guard."

The mention of the King's Guard piqued her curiosity. "And? Did he make it?"

"Don't know. Haven't heard from him since." He nodded as he considered his tankard. "I can't see any reason why he wouldn't. Pollard, that's his name. He's a giant."

Larina had been sipping on her mead. She spit the contents in her mouth back into the mug. "A giant?"

He frowned at her reaction. "Yes. Why's that so funny?"

"You, my big bear, are a giant. I can't imagine anyone bigger than you. Except maybe the brute that travels with Korwynn."

Bear smiled. "Tiny?"

"Ya, that's him. Now there's a giant if I ever saw one. I felt like a five-year-old around him."

"Tiny would be properly named in Pollard's presence, let me tell ya. The son of Thoril is a true giant. Must stand at least a foot taller than Tiny, *and* he's all muscle."

Larina smiled and took a drink; raising her eyebrows twice suggestively. "I wouldn't mind meeting this Pollard fellow."

"Ya, well, I dare say he would have nothing to do with the likes of you…" He held up a hand. "Or me! Pollard is an honourable man."

Larina feigned hurt feelings. “I’m honourable.”

“You know what I mean. Besides, this city was founded by his ancestors. Just because Storms End has fallen into disrepute doesn’t change the fact that the Banebridges are nothing but people of the highest pedigree. Pollard left because he no longer wishes to be associated with the present-day leadership of the city.”

“So, then, what’s the matter with me accepting the job?” She lowered her voice. “Do you know how much good I can do with three hundred gold?”

“The money’s no good to you dead.”

“Come on. Don’t talk like that. Ain’t no one gonna catch the Lightning Bolt.”

“And that’s another thing. You’re getting cocky.”

She mulled over his words as she finished her drink. Placing the tankard on the table, an inner warmth flooded her as she admired Bear’s fuzzy face watching her with concern. She smiled and patted his hand. “I’ll be careful. I promise. If everything goes well, this will be my last job. Once I get paid, I won’t have to steal again.”

Bear remained silent for a while, holding her gaze. He cupped her hands and squeezed.

If she wasn’t mistaken, tears threatened to form in his eyes.

“Look, Bolt. Banebridge Manor isn’t like anything you’ve ever seen before. Old man Thoril held a high position in the Royal Guard before King Peter was killed. Not sure what his role was, but rumour is he almost singlehandedly took on Helleden’s army.”

Larina raised skeptical eyebrows.

Bear shrugged. “That’s what I heard. Anyway, he may be old, but I wouldn’t want to confront him without a real bear at my back. You hear me?”

Larina

She squeezed his hand. "I said I'll be careful. I don't see what the big deal is."

"The big deal *is*, Thoril Banebridge represents everything you have striven to champion in the streets. I met the man. Honour. Integrity. Benevolence. Kindness. Compassion. These are the words people will utter over his grave. I don't like the fact that you're getting involved in wronging him. I wish you'd reconsider."

"This was your idea!"

"Before I knew who the target was. Had I known, I would never have involved you. Judging by what Korwynn and that Cyello fellow claim, and I can back up their information, it'll take an army just to get inside. The gods only know how well the scroll is guarded."

"It's a scroll. I doubt anyone pays attention to it."

"I wouldn't be so sure. If they're willing to pay four hundred gold, I imagine its worth a lot more than that."

"Three hundred," she corrected.

"The original price was four. If I have the way of it, they were willing to pay more. Be careful, Bolt. There's more to this scroll than we know."

Bear had said that before. She hadn't given it much thought, but for some reason the relevance started to bother her. Searching for something to say to defend her decision to carry on with the job, she said, "If old man Thoril is such a good man, why hasn't he done anything about the conditions in the upper tiers?"

"Perhaps he isn't aware of them."

"Come on." Her voice raised. "He's the freaking Master of Storms End. He heads up the council. How could he not know?"

Bear sighed. "Beats me. He's only one voice. If the other members of the council are in league with the baron, there's probably not much he can do."

Larina signalled a barmaid for two more tankards and brooded until she paid the woman and watched her walk away. Staring at the froth topping her ale, she bit at her lower lip. The more she considered the morality of what she was about to undertake, the more it troubled her. And yet, regardless of how she or Bear felt, there were the lives of the displaced citizens to consider. Like it or not, even if she could back out, she knew in her heart she wouldn't. People were suffering. Their situation was only going to get worse as the summer faded into autumn.

She took a deep swallow. Wiping her lips on her cuff, she burped. "Ain't nothing to be done about it now. I've gone and spent a chunk of the down payment."

Bear lowered his mug. "I'll pay for what you used. Please. Don't do this."

"You have a couple gold pieces kicking around?"

"A couple? What did you buy?" He held up his hand. "Wait. Don't tell me. Whatever you need, I'll get it, and we can return their money."

She held his gaze. As much good as the money could do for her friends, she had also been experiencing misgivings. Especially after Korwynn had explained how difficult the job would be. She couldn't recall ever fretting over the details of a heist, but something about this one unnerved her. Inherent danger was always a player—it wasn't that. Perhaps the fact that she tended to agree with Bear about the scruples of being involved in a caper that had her stealing from one of Storms End's most respected citizens.

The tavern door burst open and three men stormed in.

Larina

Larina jumped, but it wasn't the Watch that frightened her. Ambling like an overstuffed troll, Tiny cleared a path across the floor toward them; Korwynn and Cyello in tow. She squeezed Bear's forearm. "Leave them to me."

"Ah, just the two people we're looking for."

Larina and Bear nodded as the men assumed a seat on the bench across the table.

Larina poised to speak, but Cyello cut her off. "We need to move up the heist."

She blinked; the words she wanted to speak stuck in her throat. Instead, she asked, "Why? I need time to prepare."

Korwynn leaned across the table. "Let's just say that a certain bit of important information has come to our attention. If we don't do it tonight, we may lose the opportunity."

Larina tried to hold his menacing gaze but couldn't. She exchanged looks with Bear who raised his eyebrows. Anger welled up inside her. Narrowing her eyes, she met Korwynn's stare. "What's this *we*? I'm the one going over the wall."

"We'll be creating the diversion, remember?"

"Big deal. Brutes like you, hooting and hollering at the gate while I attempt to slip past an army of trained killers."

"That was the deal you agreed to when you accepted the advance. Perhaps you'd like to give it back and we'll find someone else, hmm?" Korwynn's dark glare intimated that he knew she had spent some of the money.

She tried to buy time to think of a way out. "Do you realize who the man is that we're taking the scroll from?"

The three men exchanged looks. Korwynn's hands shot out and clutched her wrists and pulled; doubling her over the table.

Bear stiffened, his hand going to his dagger, but Tiny and Cyello already had theirs in hand.

Korwynn ignored Bear and bent low to growl in her ear. "What of Thoril Banebridge? Is there something you want to tell me?"

She tried to pull away but his iron grip held her fast. "No, but—"

"But nothing, Miss Bolt. You're either with us or…" His eyes invited her to look at Cyello and Tiny poised to strike.

"Leave Bear out of this. It's between you and me."

"It's between whoever I say it is." Korwynn sneered. "You get me?"

She nodded.

Korwynn released her and sat back.

Rubbing her chafed wrists, Larina glared at the curious faces in the tavern watching the commotion.

One look from Tiny, and they returned to their own business.

The outer door flew open. Rock followed a concerned barmaid into the room. Scanning the tavern, he located their table and started forward but a subtle shake of Bear's head stopped him. Rock appeared to weigh the situation as he strolled to the bar and ordered a drink; never taking his eyes from their table.

An evil grin split Korwynn's face. "I suggest your friend over there remains out of this if you get my meaning."

Larina swallowed. She didn't doubt Bear's ability, and with Rock to back them up, she was fairly confident they were a match for the three strangers, but something about Korwynn gave her pause. She prided herself in reading people and what she saw in the dark-haired brute scared her more than she cared to admit.

"Well? Are you in, or not?"

She glowered at Korwynn, her breaths coming in ragged spurts.

"Or should we seek out a certain old man in the upper city and have words with him?"

Larina's mouth fell open before she could stop it.

"Aye. One of the old guard, that one. Be a shame if something unfortunate were to befall, Sir Allard."

Larina forced angered words through closed teeth, her hands clenching and unclenching in rage. "If you lay a hand on him, I'll slit your throat with *his* dagger." She indicated Tiny with a flick of her eyes.

Rock stepped away from the bar.

Bear prepared to slide out from between the table; matching Cyello's movement.

Korwynn belted out a hearty laugh. "Hah! I don't doubt you for a second. And what a joy it would be to behold. Alas, I have no time to be the recipient of your idle threats. Either return my money, or call off your dogs and walk out of here with us. Your choice."

Larina sighed. "Fine. I'm in."

She held up a finger and waved it at Rock. "We're good."

Rock stared hard, as if trying to read a hidden meaning in her gesture.

She gave him a subtle shake of her head.

It wasn't until he dipped his chin and strolled out the door that she felt she could breathe again.

Larina

Strange Revelation

Bear accompanied Larina as they led her employers up the steep zig-zagging streets meandering the heights of the fjord. Making their way through the destroyed upper tier and into the posh district beyond; large estates sprawled along the top of the cliff face affording their owners a commanding view of the countryside.

If not for the adrenaline surging through her veins, Larina would have fretted over her lack of sleep the last few days; not to mention her tired muscles that hadn't had time to recover from her recent adventure at the watchtower. The pent-up exhilaration of flirting with disaster kept her feet trudging up the hillside—that and her concern that she needed to hurry for Allard and the other's sake.

She couldn't help worrying about the Watch retaliating; hitting her where it hurt worst. The farther she climbed, the more she feared that if she didn't go to them immediately, they wouldn't be alive by the time she returned. Stealing the scroll would likely take her the better part of the night.

Korwynn, Tiny, and Cyello stomped along a few steps behind Larina and Bear. The strangers spoke in hushed voices, unintelligible to either of them as they crested a steep rise and started along the uppermost tier of Storms End.

She knew the city well. Beyond the small temple at the end of the street, a roadway would take them to the walls surrounding Banebridge Manor.

Larina

Without considering the ramifications of her rashness, she stepped ahead and spun about, her dagger in hand. "I can't do this."

Before Korwynn or his lackeys could say anything, she elaborated. “At least, not until I check on my friends.”

Swords slid free of their scabbards.

Bear positioned himself between her and Korwynn’s crew as they fanned out.

Not for the first time, Larina wished she had a better weapon than a dagger. The small blade had served her well skulking about in places she shouldn’t, but she rarely found herself in the open, facing swordsmen. On the few occasions she had, she’d taken to the rooftops and eluded them.

The fact that she even thought of doing that now filled her with guilt. Korwynn’s men would cut Bear down in the street without thinking twice.

She tried to step around Bear but he held her back with an outstretched arm. “Easy lass. Let me deal with them.”

She stepped back and sideways, but Bear moved his bulk to keep her behind him. “Please, Bolt. I can’t fight you *and* them.” His fingers wrapped themselves in her tunic below her neck and held fast.

“Leave Bear out of this!” She tried to pry his fingers off her clothing but she might as well have tried to move a mountain. “Bear! Let go!”

Korwynn approached Bear with his black warhammer held in both hands. “For the love of hell, it’s too late for that, Miss Bolt. Your friend…” He looked at the buildings flanking the cobblestone street. “…*all* your friends are involved now. If you decide to back out, there’ll be serious repercussions.”

“I’m not backing out.” Larina twisted and pulled in Bear’s grasp, nearly pulling her tunic over her head in her struggle to break his grip.

Just before he unshirted her, Bear released her.

She took a moment to straighten her clothing. Whipping her hair about to get it to settle, she sidestepped Bear and approached Korwynn. Cyello kept a wary blade hovering close to the small of her back.

"I need to check on someone. I may have put him and a few others in harm's way."

"Ain't our problem."

"When I agreed to do this, you said it wouldn't happen until tomorrow night."

"Things change."

She raised a cocky eyebrow and held her free hand toward Bear. "Ya? Well, that ain't *our* problem."

"It is if you wish to get paid. The scroll will be harder to steal after tonight. Likely impossible."

She frowned, lowering her dagger. "Why's that?"

"Ain't your concern. You've been paid more than most people make in a lifetime. If you wish to keep it and get the rest, I suggest you tell your friend to lower his sword and start walking."

The way Korwynn held his warhammer suggested he knew how to use it. Cyello and Tiny weren't looking too concerned either. It was her fault Bear was in this position. She should have talked him out of accompanying her from the *Kraken's Curse*. She would never forgive herself if something happened to him.

A sly grin crossed Korwynn's face. "If I'm right, perhaps you'll change your mind when I tell you this. What we're trying to obtain by stealing the scroll is a way to undermine the very people you fight so hard against with your petty game of cat and mouse. If you do as we ask and retrieve the scroll, you'll help us bring down the establishment."

Larina thought long and hard, weighing her options after listening to Korwynn's strange revelation. The more she mulled it over, the more she realized there really was only one choice that made sense. She sheathed her dagger and faced Bear. "It's okay. Put your sword away."

Bear swallowed, his dark scowl flitting from one man to the next.

"Save it for another day," Larina said softly. "I need you to do something for me."

"He ain't going nowhere," Cyello growled.

"Oh yeah?" Larina spun on him, her dagger appearing in her hand like magic. She knew she was taking a big gamble. "If he's not allowed to go, then I'm done."

"Not bloody—"

Korwynn shouldered his hammer and held up a staying hand. "Fine. The fat one can go. But…" He pointed at Bear's face. "If you try anything covert, I promise you, the Bolt will pay with her life. You get me?"

Bear bladed his stance; his sword poised to strike.

For a tense moment, Larina feared Bear would try to take advantage of Korwynn's shouldered weapon.

She put a gloved hand on Bear's blade and forced it down. "I need you to check on Allard. Can you do that for me?"

Bear kept his eyes on Korwynn. "I'm not leaving you alone with these people."

She stepped past his sword and hugged him. "You're a true friend. You know I love you, but right now, I need you to trust me. Let me do this. They obviously want the scroll badly. I'll be fine."

"I'm not leaving you alone with them."

She squeezed him harder. "You can and you will. I can't concentrate on what I have to do if I'm worrying about Allard and the others. Knowing that you're seeing to their safety, I'll be able to get this over with quickly and then we'll all be happy."

Bear's glare moved from one man to another. He sighed and Larina felt his muscles release their tension. He returned her embrace; his mass engulfing her slight frame.

She felt him kiss the top of her head. Leaning her head back, she gazed into his warm eyes, sad to see him fighting back tears. She squeezed him and let go. "Allard's on the third floor of the old magistrate's building. Do you know where that is?"

"Aye."

"Get him, and anyone else, out of there. Find a safe place and stay with them. Send word to the *Curse* and I'll find you when this is done. Now go."

Bear hesitated. Cyello and Tiny maintained their vigilant posturing, as if inviting him to attack.

"Bear," Larina drew out his name, pleading for him to listen. "Keep my people safe for me. I'm counting on you."

He forced a smile for her benefit. With slouched shoulders he waddled toward the hill, giving Tiny a wide berth.

"Oh yes. I almost forgot," Korwynn interrupted her concentration on her friend. He produced a flattened, suede tube. "Put the scroll in this to protect it."

She absently accepted the tube. Korwynn's gesture reminded her of her own burden she needed to be rid of if she planned to be as quiet as the moon's passage. She stepped between Korwynn and Tiny, and called after Bear, "Wait!"

Bear turned fast, raising his sword and looking for trouble.

"Here." Larina pulled the bag of coins from where she kept it hidden at her waist and tossed it to him. "Watch this for me. I'll be wanting it back sooner than you know."

Bear caught the bag; its contents jingling.

"Be safe," was all he said. A resigned sigh followed him over the crest of the hill and out of sight.

Larina

Over the Wall

Balancing on Tiny's shoulders, Larina's mind swirled with misgivings of how wrong everything she was about to undertake felt in her gut. Not one to balk at danger, nor waste conscious thought on the right or wrong of stealing from society's well-to-do in order to assist those that life had left in the midden pile and forgot, something about stealing a document from the Master of the Storms End Council screamed at her as a bad idea.

Her boots planted firmly on the giant man's shoulders, she stretched to her toes and grasped the top of a lichen covered stone wall. Without the brute to hoist her to the top of the perimeter wall lining the Banebridge Manor estate, she doubted she would have been able to scale the slick surface. Even with his assistance, her gloved hands found it difficult to find purchase on the overgrowth.

"Ya gonna lollygag all night?" Tiny's high-pitched voice called up to her

"Why? Am I too heavy for you?" She whispered harshly, conscious of being overheard on the far side of the wall.

"Och, lass. You weigh no more 'n me supper. It's just that I need to get to the gate before Korwynn and Cyello are spotted."

His words gave her pause. She frowned down at him, unseen by the brute. "Are you serious?" Her breath vapour escaped her lips in a cloud. "No one's going to be out on a miserable night like this. Your mates can strip naked and run around to their heart's content and I doubt they'll attract more attention than a bored night owl."

He grumbled something incoherent.

Shaking her head, she admonished, "Just keep steady while I scan the yard to see what I have to deal with."

The stone wall disappeared in both directions into the mist rising off the moors lining the top of the fjord. Black sentinels surrounded the stretch of rolling land beyond, shooting into the sky not far from where she perched as the northern reaches of the Spine Mountain Range dominated the skyline in every direction.

A large building, resplendent with terraced balconies and encircled by meandering pathways that passed between fountains, statues, and meticulously manicured bushes, was barely visible through the thick mist.

At first, she didn't see anyone out and about but after careful observation, a shadow separated itself from a large statue fronting what she assumed was the main egress into Banebridge Manor. The person, who she could only assume was a guard, strolled toward where she suspected the front gate lay. She held her breath, not daring to tell Tiny. Korwynn and Cyello should be there by now.

Another silhouette appeared from out of the mist around the front corner of the building. The first figure stopped and turned. It was obvious they spoke to each other but their words were muted by distance and thick fog.

The first guard strolled to where the second one waited. Together, they disappeared around the broad entrance steps.

Larina released a long breath and gathered her wits. It was time to steal a scroll.

Tiny grunted as she bent at the knees and sprung onto the top of the wall, landing on her stomach. The lichen, still wet from the earlier storm, soaked through her tunic and the thighs of her leather breeks. Ignoring the discomfort, she searched the grounds. No one was visible through the mist.

She ensured the space at the base of the twelve-foot wall was clear, and dropped onto the lawn without a sound. Doubled over, she ran to the nearest bush and ducked behind its cover. Breath vapour escaped her mouth in rapid puffs. If anything was going to give her away, she feared the cold, night air would be her undoing.

From what Korwynn and Cyello had told her, there should have been more than two guards patrolling the grounds. Not leaving anything to chance, she took her time scanning the interior of the perimeter wall. There wasn't much to see in the mist shrouded darkness. A full-grown person could be standing twenty paces away and she wouldn't see them.

For some inexplicable reason, she thought about the female archer from the other night. The woman's strange appearance had given Larina the willies. Sure, the woman may just be a new recruit in the Storms End Watch, but Larina doubted that was the case. The woman was too good to be new. Too good to be content at being part of the city guard. The woman was a professional.

Larina shook her head to clear her thoughts. She'd have to worry about the archer another day. Tonight, she needed her full concentration to pull off what appeared on paper as a near impossible heist. Impossible for someone not used to making themselves invisible. Not impossible for her.

Clad in supple black leather from head to toe, she darted across the expansive grounds—flitting from shadow to shadow; her movement no louder than a butterfly's breath.

She darted across a well-maintained path that meandered through the grounds between manicured shrubbery and beautiful pieces of standing stonework shaped in all sorts of various creatures. Small turtles and frogs. Song birds and falcons. Rabbits and racoons. Deer and predatory cats. Horses and dragons. Judging by the encrusted lichen, the magnificent statues were centuries old.

With her back against the thick trunk of an ancient maple, she eased her way around it until she had a clear view of the front entranceway. The fact that neither of the guards had returned concerned her. She would be more comfortable sneaking around if she knew where they were.

The yellow stone of the large, three-storied manse loomed overhead; sprawling into the mist toward its rear. According to the roughly sketched plans Cyello had shown her in the *Kraken's Curse*, there were two main floor entrances—one on each end of the house. Those were reportedly watched over by a least one guard, day and night. If dispatched expertly enough, she would be able to get past one and sneak inside, but if there was more than one, she would be hard put to deal with them both.

She had scoffed at Korwynn's initial concern; assuring him that the Storms End Lightning Bolt rarely entered a building by conventional means.

Broad balconies extended from the second and third floors in no apparent order—magnificently worked, stone-carved balustrades lining their unique shapes. That was how she planned to enter the building unnoticed, but first, she had to locate the wandering guards. It wouldn't do to have them catch her in the middle of scaling the walls to reach the balconies above.

Her blood ran cold.

Someone coughed from where she had dropped over the outer wall. She pressed her body against the trunk and crept around its girth until she could see the dark presence of the outer wall through the gloom. Of the person who had coughed, there was no sign.

A hearty laugh split the night air. Rounding the front of the homestead, two men strolled into the open bearing polearms, and outfitted with boiled leather armour embossed with plate at the elbows and shoulders. Long sheaths hung from wide belts, above knee-high boots that were buffed to a shine and refracted what little light filtered through the overcast sky.

Trapped between the two guards in view and the one she couldn't locate, Larina fought to control her breathing. If she were spotted, she would be hard-pressed to find a way over the wall.

As she debated her options, a whiff of pipe smoke caught her attention. She originally assumed it came from the men out front, but neither one appeared to hold anything in their hands.

She slowly turned her head to face the wall. If the person who had coughed was smoking a pipe, the glow from the bowl should give him away.

"Ah, Lars," an elderly voice right on top of her made her jerk her head back to the manse.

"'Tis a nasty night to be watching over an old man. Come into the library for a warm mug." The voice came from a balcony that projected into the edge of the great maple's boughs.

Larina tried to shrink down and look through the leafy branches, but wasn't able to see anything. She hoped the same was true for whoever stood above her. The closeness of the boughs to the building gave her an idea.

"Ah, Master Thoril." A deeper, younger voice responded. "I would love nothing more, but you know I cannot. If your son ever found out I shirked my duty, well…you know."

"Bah. Don't worry about him. He's not like me or his grandfather. He's pretty mild-mannered. Though, I guess I wouldn't want to upset him. I've been told he fights like the Kraidic Crusher."

"Exactly my point, sir."

"Not to worry. He's not expected to arrive until sometime tomorrow."

"Ha, ha. I'd rather not take any chances. Thank you, though. It's very kind of you to offer."

"Suit yourself. Goodnight then."

"Goodnight sir."

Larina's wide eyes searched the dark boughs, but it was no use. The muted squeal of hinges disturbed the night, followed by a hollow thud. The Master of Storms End had retired for the night.

A shadow materialized out of the fog, casually strolling along the path she had skirted. If not for the fact that no one was aware of her presence, she figured her dark form pressed against the tree would have stood out as plain as day.

She willed the man to keep walking toward the other two, but the parting clouds overhead made her breath catch. Brilliant moonlight flooded the grounds, illuminating the bearded face of the lone guard ambling straight at her—his head lifting to gaze at the tree.

Larina

The Prize

"Guards!"

The lone guard's eyes grew wide.

"To me!"

Larina fought to keep her heart from racing as the guard ran at her; passing the maple on the far side and storming onto the gravel path that led from the estate's front entranceway toward a massive, wrought-iron gate in the wall somewhere beyond the low-lying mist.

Barely able to breathe, Larina eased around the trunk, keeping the tree between her and the charging guard. She started to lean out to follow him as he ran into the mist, but froze when out of nowhere, from the back of the nearside of the mansion, two men hurried past the maple to join the chase.

She swallowed and carefully surveyed the grounds. Her gaze drifted to the balcony where she had heard Thoril and the house guard. She had a clear view of it now. Thankfully, whoever had been stationed up there hadn't stayed by the railing. In all of the uproar, she had nearly made a fatal mistake.

A smile crossed her face as she realized what was happening. Korwynn and his men were providing the distraction she required to slip unannounced into Banebridge Manor. Taking a last look around, she assessed a way up the trunk of the maple to the lowest bough. With a mighty leap she scrambled up the folds of the old bark and wrapped an arm around the base of a thick branch. Agile as a mountain lion, she pulled herself onto it and bounded along its massive girth; skirting around smaller boughs that branched off on either side.

She paused every few steps to ensure no one remained on the balcony stretching out to meet her. The branch began to bend as she neared its end. Two quick steps and a short leap and she landed without a sound on the flagstone balcony floor inside the thick balustrade.

From her new vantage point, she could hear the slightest of commotions in the distance. She could only imagine what antics Korwynn and his men were up to—the thickening mist making it impossible to see beyond the front corner of the building. If anyone lingered around the house, they would be nearly impossible to spot, but she had no time to worry about it. If someone had seen her, she would know soon enough.

Indecision held her in her crouch. A secret longing had her hoping to see Korwynn and his lackeys being paraded up the walkway in irons—or better yet, witnessing their lifeless bodies being dragged up to the entrance. If that were to happen, she would be over the balcony railing and gone faster than a troll fled daylight.

Against her better judgement, she lingered; waiting to see if her wishes might come true. A little voice in the back of her mind screamed at her to get moving—that the distraction wouldn't last forever. Once it was over, the homestead would be crawling with returning guardsmen—their senses heightened.

Most of the visible windows were dark, but a few flickered with soft candle glow. She traced the sweeping curves of the balcony that spanned most of this side of the house, and noted two large doorways at either end. Though she hadn't seen old man Banebridge, he had mentioned something about a library. He had no sooner finished speaking than door hinges squealed and the thump of a door closing had marked his departure. If he had retired to the library to have the drink he spoke of, she surmised the room must be closer to this end of the house.

Putting aside her faint hopes of not having to go through with Korwynn's caper, the voice of reason got the better of her. If she didn't move soon, her chance of pulling it off would be lost. So would the extra two hundred gold coins she was promised. Nor did she have any delusions that her employers would allow her to hang onto the down payment. If that was the case, her life would revert to what it had always been. A daily struggle of hardship and survival.

Her leather gloves creaked as she clenched her fists. Bear's words haunted her. *'You're getting cocky.'*

Perhaps he was right. At some point, no matter how good she thought she was, someone would catch her.

She snorted her derision. It had almost happened twice in the last couple of days. First with the archer and then at the watchtower.

She could see Bear's condescending face as they dragged her away in irons to be publicly flogged before they stretched her neck at the town gallows. He would shake his head and tell her he had told her so. About what, though, she couldn't be sure—her brashness, or her insistence to take this job. Likely both.

'The money's no good to you dead,' echoed through her mind as she sized up her approach to the nearest door.

She did her best to shake free of those annoying voices, and straightened her lithe form to its full height. Quiet as a ghost's shadow, she slunk around the contours of the yellow stone wall and approached a wide set of double doors.

The yellow glow of a low-flaming sconce on the other side of multiple panes of glass comprising the entryway allowed Larina to snatch a quick look inside before attempting the brass door lever. Floor to ceiling shelves filled with books lined the walls of a two-story room. A thin balcony surrounded the perimeter of the room halfway up the wall—reached by at least one wrought-iron, circular stairwell providing access to thousands of tomes higher up.

Sculpted, dark wood tables sat scattered amongst several, high-backed, cushioned chairs—their chiselled arms and masterfully formed legs worthy of a monarch's throne. From her vantage point, no one appeared to be in the library.

She cast a look around the balcony to ensure she hadn't missed anything. Satisfied, she retrieved a tiny leather pouch from an inner pocket and pulled its cute stopper free. The end of the oil pouch was thin enough to slip between the door and the frame. With the softest of pressure, she squeezed a drop of lubricant onto the upper hinge. Locating the lower hinge, she repeated the procedure. She replaced the stopper and put the pouch away before easing the handle of the door down. It stopped part way. Locked.

Undeterred, her fingers rummaged through another small leather pouch hidden beneath her tunic, and fished out a flat piece of steel covered with nocks and bumps and a slight hook at one end. Inserting it into the keyhole, she deftly worked the lock pick until the tumblers moved beneath her sensitive touch. The door handle pushed all the way down and the door opened without a sound.

It had taken her no longer than several breaths to gain access into one of the heaviest guarded estates in all of Storms End. To Larina, with the exception of the close call on the grounds below, it had been no more difficult than lacing up the thongs of her boots over her leather breeks to keep the bottoms from swishing together as she snuck around.

A smug smile lifted her cheeks as she stepped across the threshold into Banebridge Manor and softly closed the door behind her. There was good reason people referred to her as the Lightning Bolt.

Tip-toeing across thick broadloom, she grabbed a handheld candle holder and lit it from the single sconce burning on a wide panel between bookshelves. She waited for her eyes to accustom themselves to the sudden brightness, and scanned the large room, fretting that the scroll could be anywhere. Her gaze lingered on a smoked-glass dome dominating a small table in the middle of a long wall that separated two interior doors.

She frowned. It couldn't be that easy.

A floorboard creaked from beyond one of the two doors interrupting the library shelves.

She fingered the hilt of her dagger, but wasn't keen on using it. Killing innocent people, even if they were guards intent on capturing her, wasn't her style. If they decided to attack, that was a different matter.

A tall, iron candlestick caught her eye. She placed her candle on the table beside the dome. Snapping the partially burnt candle from the top of the candlestick, she hoisted it with two hands, appreciating its heft.

Another floorboard creaked—closer.

Judging by the hinges, the door opened outward. A frantic search for somewhere to hide led her to crouch behind one of the two thronelike chairs on either side of the domed table.

Larina

The door creaked open and a tall, black haired, clean-shaven young man entered the room bearing an oil-burning lamp. He stopped and frowned at the candle Larina had lit.

Taking a moment to scan the room, he muttered, “That’s odd,” and strode over to the table. He scratched his head and bent down to blow out the flickering candle. “Not like him to leave an open flame unattend—”

Larina struck hard. The sound of the metal candlestick cracking the back of the man’s head made her wince as he collapsed ever so slowly to the carpet in front of the domed table.

His lamp hit the thick broadloom, still clutched in his hand, and tipped over, spilling oil, but its glass chimney remained intact.

She pounced on the lamp before it had a chance to ignite the carpet, all the while fearing she might have killed him.

In the warm glow of his lamp, she noticed a nasty lump at the base of his skull but his chest falls reassured her he lived.

Her gaze flitted between the inner doors, fearing someone might have heard the brief commotion, but the manor remained deathly still.

Not wasting time, she put the lamp beside her burning candle and inspected the dome. It was difficult to see what lay beneath the glass cover, but she couldn’t help notice the etched dragon surrounding the dome’s rim.

She mused that it wasn’t a typical dragon. It didn’t have wings. Looking closer, she realized it didn’t have appendages at all. The worm-like dragon’s mouth held a small circle of red glass clutched between fangs—a long, forked tongue curled underneath the gemlike depiction and protruded over its hind section as the image came full-circle.

The dome itself had no handle with which to lift it. Wary, she inspected the glass where it met the table’s edge for signs of a trap—she had suffered harm on more than one occasion from a booby-trapped item.

She knelt and bent her shoulder to the ground, waving the small candle underneath the tabletop, but couldn't detect anything untoward.

Holding her breath, she placed her damp gloves against the dome and lifted the heavy glass—her face scrunched up in anticipation of feeling something cut into her, but nothing happened. Carefully depositing the dome on the chair beside her, she couldn't take her eyes off the yellow roll of parchment sitting atop a delicate cradle and held tight by a cracked and faded leather thong.

She hesitated reaching for it, fearing it might crumble at her touch. To grab it and slip it into the suede tube Korwynn had given her would have been her best choice, but curiosity made her long to know what was worth four hundred gold coins. The fact that she had allowed herself to be talked down to three hundred still vexed her, but she knew that even that much gold was more than enough to accomplish everything she dreamed of and then some.

She removed her gloves and set them beside the dome. Ever so careful, she grasped the dangling ends of the simple knot and tugged. The leather strips broke off in her hands.

The silence in the chamber thundered in her head. Other than her hammering heartbeat, the hiss of the oil lamp and the low burning wall sconce were the only sounds disturbing the well-insulated room.

She swallowed, afraid of what might happen if she attempted to remove the remaining scraps of thong that had crumbled in her fingers. She shrugged and thought, *'Why not?'* If the scroll fell apart, how would Korwynn know it was her doing?

Larina

Holding her breath, she flicked the bits from the scroll's surface and laid the prize beside its cradle. The edges of the scroll tore slightly in her grasp but thankfully held together as she unrolled it. Mesmerized, she tried to make sense of what was pictured there.

A roughly drawn map of mountains bordering a body of water at the top of the scroll. A faint, dotted line—smudged in several places—meandered along the bottom of the map, below the mountains, until it reached a certain point and headed to the base of one mountain in particular.

Odd sayings, looking like they were written after the fact by a different stylus and hue of ink, riddled the map in different places. She mused they were notations to assist the memory of the bearer as she read them. *Mase's Legacy. The Eye of the mountain sits atop a seemingly unscalable cliff. Search out the handholds. The bowels of Gimcrack.*

Completely absorbed in trying to understand what she was looking at, she didn't hear the faint squeak of a floorboard from the opposite direction to where the guard had entered.

A hinge squealed. Icy tendrils of fear crept up her spine as a man's voice filled the chamber. "Lars, is that you?"

Larina

Senile Lunatic

Larina's head whipped around to stare into the wrinkled visage of a stoop-shouldered man beneath a full head of long, grey hair.

The man gasped, holding an age-spotted hand over his mouth, but instead of sounding the alarm, he shuffled to where Larina bent over the table holding the scroll stretched out.

He frowned at the guard unconscious behind her. "My word. What's happened?"

Larina didn't know what to do. If the person confronting her had been anyone but somebody who appeared to already have one foot in the grave, she would have snatched up the scroll, drove a fist into his face, and stole away.

"Is he dead?"

Larina carefully helped the scroll to curl back on itself, and stood. "No, sir. He'll have a headache when he comes to, but he'll be fine."

"And who are you, young lady? What're you doing in my house?" He squinted at the scroll in her hands—his faded black robe clinging to the angular frame it hid beneath. "And what do you think you're doing with the Crusher Scroll?"

Crusher Scroll? The name of the document in her hand echoed through her mind. An odd sense of guilt muddied her ability to think straight. It wasn't like her to freeze under stress. She had made her name by reacting under pressure, but for some reason, the old man's presence left her speechless.

"Do you know what you have in your hands?"

She shook her head. Recovering from her initial shock, she held his pale, blue-eyed gaze as she eased the suede tube from where she had tucked it in her belt, and worried its edges into a round shape to accommodate the scroll.

"You hold the key to unlock Zephyr's demise."

She frowned at the scroll; regarding it like she held a snake. It was all she could do not to drop it.

The old man nodded. "Aye. In the wrong hands, the Crusher Scroll will prove devastating. It holds the key to destroy the entire kingdom."

She frowned. "It's just a map."

He raised a single, bushy eyebrow. "Just a map to you, dear child. But, in the right hands, it will provide the bearer the means to locate a power greater than anything you can imagine."

The price the men were willing to pay for it began to make sense.

"I don't believe you. Magic is gone from the land."

"How quickly you young ones forget. Queen Quarrnaine and many courageous souls gave their lives to save us from this so-called lack of magic. You must have heard about how the sky turned cinder and fire rained down on the land?"

"Yes, but Helleden's dead. He was the last of the magic users."

"So quick to judge. That's the trouble with today's society. No one takes the time to seek the truth. You've been lulled into a false sense of security. Easier to accept that the world will go on the way it is without a care, than expend unnecessary energy coming to terms with the fact that someday soon…"

Appearing flustered at his inability to find the right words to finish his sentence, he pointed a shaky finger; his voice deepening. "Let me tell you, young lady. There's a storm brewing over the ocean. A big one. If the ache in my bones tells me true, we're staring the end of times in the face."

She gaped at him as if he were a senile lunatic. Not wanting to consider his preposterous claim, she changed the subject. "You're Thoril Banebridge, right?"

"What a stupid question! Who else would I be? Of course, I'm Thoril Banebridge." He shook his head in disgust and sat down—easing his stick-like body into the chair on the far side of the domed table.

Her gaze searched out the old man's other hand. His last two fingers and a good part of his hand were missing. She swallowed and forced herself to look him in the eye, thinking how bizarre it felt to carry on a conversation with the person she was stealing from.

Her eyes widened. The cagey, old man was stalling her. She cautiously tightened the scroll until it slid comfortably into the suede tube.

She poised to flee, but Thoril reminded her so much of Allard, that guilt held her back. "Look, Master Banebridge. I feel bad about stealing your scroll, but I have no choice."

Thoril's tired eyes narrowed. Somewhere, deep within his gaze, she could see the essence of the powerful man he once was. The sight made her shudder.

"As long as one draws breath, there's always a choice." Thoril's shaky voice turned dark and menacing. "You feel bad about taking something that doesn't belong to you, hmm? The key that will give the bearer access to an artifact powerful enough to cause thousands of senseless deaths and expedite the ruin of the world. You've a strange way of demonstrating remorse. If you leave with that map, you'll bring Zephyr to its knees."

She had stepped over Lars and was heading for the balcony door. His words stopped her. She turned to face his resigned expression. Holding the suede tube out between them, she said, "So you keep saying. This looks like a treasure map. I fail to see how it can take down a kingdom."

She had to strain to hear his soft reply.

"Not all treasures are golden. In your hands is the means to unlock a magic this world hasn't seen in half a millennium. One so powerful that no one can stand in its way. In the wrong hands, lives *will* be lost. Many lives."

She hesitated, debating his words. She had no way to verify anything Thoril told her. Delivering the scroll to Korwynn would provide her with the means to make a difference in so many lives. Lives that would be lost in the coming months. For her, and all the people she watched over, the storm that Thoril spoke of was already here.

Thoril's next words surprised her.

"Tell me. What do these people look like that inquire after the scroll?"

She pondered the question.

Before she could answer, Thoril added, "They're likely large, foreign men."

She shrugged. "How am I supposed to know where they're from?"

"Do they strike you as common thieves?"

That was an odd question. A question she had asked herself a few times since making their acquaintance. Even Bear had insinuated as much; his words echoed in her mind, *'...let's just say these men don't strike me as everyday criminals.'*

Larina

"Come to think of it, they *don't* strike me as common criminals." She nodded. "And yes, they're larger than normal."

Thoril sighed. "It's as I suspected. They're part of the Kraidic Initiative."

"The Kraidic what?"

"A dangerous force that aims to bring about the downfall of the free kingdoms." He nodded at her inquisitive stare. "Aye. I beg you. Reconsider what you're about to do. King Malcolm, the Learned, cannot field an army large enough to defend against the rising storm. Helleden's recent invasion has seen to that. If you provide these men with that scroll, you'll doom us all."

An awful feeling twisted her gut. She struggled to believe a word he said. He was probably speaking in circles to keep her contained until help arrived. But, if he wasn't, and events transpired as he predicted, she would be responsible for unleashing a grave catastrophe.

"Larina…" Thoril spoke her name and let it hang between them.

She stared wild-eyed. How did he know her name? She had fought so hard to keep her former life a secret. Up until last night, Bear and Rock were the only ones who knew her true identity.

He nodded. "Aye. You may not know me, but I know you. Well, I know of you. You're the Storms End Lightning Bolt. Sir Allard speaks highly of you."

Her jaw dropped; finding it hard to breathe. "How do you know Allard?"

"We fought together during King Peter's darkest hour. A finer man to watch my back, I'll never know."

"But…But…" So many questions shot through her mind, but all she could think of was her friend's struggle to survive.

"Do you realize how badly this man who watched your back suffers?" She gestured around the lavish library. "While you live a life of luxury?"

She wasn't certain, but she thought Thoril's eyes moistened.

His distant gaze stared at the balcony doors. "I'm aware."

She stormed across the room and pointed the tube at him. "How do you sleep at night?"

He turned; his intense glare boring into her soul. "With one eye open to defend against the likes of you."

She held his stare. If he weren't so old, she might have throttled him. Realizing she was squeezing the tube harder than was prudent, she put it inside her tunic to free her hands, and pointed a bare finger at him. "Ya? Well, while you sit there looking all mighty and important, the man who watched your back is about to be put to the sword."

If her words had any affect on Thoril, his face didn't reflect it.

"Do you understand what I'm saying?"

"I may be old, but I'm not stupid. Allard will be fine."

"How can you know that? You don't even know where he is."

"The old magistrate's building. Third floor. The one without the broken window."

If not for the high-backed chair next to her, Larina would have dropped to the ground. "You know?"

"I'm the Master of Storms End. It's my business to know."

"Ya, well…" She patted her tunic where she placed the scroll. "You didn't know about the plan to steal this, did you?"

"No. Unfortunately, that escaped me."

"Why do you allow your friend to live in squalor."

Thoril shrugged. "His choice."

"His choice? You think he likes sleeping in maggot-infested alleyways, fending off goblin-sized rats, and worrying about the Watch sticking a blade in his gut?"

"I'm sure there are parts of his decision to shun my offer of aid that doesn't agree with him."

She was poised to go off on a tirade, but his words stopped her. "I-I don't understand. Did you say you offered to help him?"

"Aye. Every time I see the damned fool."

He made it sound like he visited Allard often. She had a hard time believing that. "And he refuses you?"

"Aye. Too much pride in that thick head. Thinks he's fighting the good fight by enduring life in the streets with the other unfortunate souls. Tells me to stuff my charity."

The fight left her. Lowering her arms, she checked on Lars before crouching at Thoril's knees; staring him in the eye. "I don't understand."

"I do, to an extent. Allard comes from a poor family. He was a brawler in his youth. His exploits in the street attracted the attention of the old baron. One thing led to another and the next thing you know, Allard ended up in Carillon, training alongside King Peter's elite guard. If not for his inability to shut his mouth on matters that were larger than himself, there was a good chance he would have made captain of the king's guard. That station would have elevated him to a peer of the realm. He would never have had to worry about a roof over his head again."

"What happened?"

"The Group of Five happened. They descended on the battlefield and dispatched Helleden Misenthorpe; ending the war. After Prince Malcolm was crowned king, the realm busied itself rebuilding. Every man, woman and child who had sought refuge at Castle Svelte was ordered to return to wherever they called home and assist in the rebuilding of Zephyr.

"Sir Allard returned to Storms End and did his part. Being a knight in the king's army, one would think his compensation would have been handsome, but after the brutal campaign, the royal coffers were stretched thin. King Malcolm couldn't afford to pay his loyal soldiers what they were worth—nor did they demand it. Well, most didn't.

"Suffice it to say, Sir Allard worked hard to rebuild Storms End for little to no pay. In the ensuing years, the older knights just..." He shrugged as he searched for what he wanted to say. "...for lack of a better word, they faded into obscurity and were forgotten. Many lived and died in the upper tiers of the city. They enjoyed a simple life and were happy for the most part.

"That all changed with Helleden's return. Our city was razed to the ground. Our biggest source of trade, the shipyards, was destroyed. Since then, Storms End hasn't been able to match the industrial might of Thunderhead and Madrigail Bay."

Larina knew most of the city's history, but she listened with rapt attention. Thoril's words explained much, but she struggled with why Thoril hadn't helped Allard or any of the others who had fallen on bad times.

"You look to be doing well for yourself. Why don't you help other people like Allard?"

The sadness returned to his eyes. "Perhaps I haven't tried hard enough. As Master of the council, I've lobbied for the rebuilding of the upper tiers but the baron has the final say. He's of the opinion that Storms End's priority lies with the defunct shipyards and the lower tiers. Only recently was I able to convince the council that the upper tiers were in dire need of rejuvenation. As a result of my urging, the baron decreed that all squatters were to be displaced." He hung his head and said softly, "That wasn't my intention, but my pleas for compassion have fallen on deaf ears."

Larina didn't know what to think. An uncomfortable silence settled over the room. Her eyes landed on her gloves. Retrieving them, she glanced at the door Lars had come through. She suspected it wouldn't be long before the guards returned.

Lars moaned at her feet. Her hand leaped to her dagger, but he remained unconscious for the moment. "I must go."

"How much are they paying you?"

She stopped in mid-stride, halfway to the balcony doors.

"I'll double it."

Her eyes widened. She could buy an estate as grand as this one.

Korwynn's menacing face flashed into the forefront of her mind—his heavy brows pinched in anger. *'...all your friends are involved now. If you decide to back out, there'll be serious repercussions.'*

What good would money be if everyone she had sacrificed so much for were dead?

She took another step and froze. Thoril's stern voice sent shivers up her spine.

"Perhaps the baron *is* right about you."

She spun, brandishing her dagger, daring him to say more.

Thoril raised his eyebrows, disappointment etched across his ancient features. "The watchtower was your doing, wasn't it? As are many other grievances our city has suffered over the past few years. The Watch have expended a lot of resources and manpower because of your exploits. Mark my words. The watchtower incident will provoke the baron into bringing the full weight of the Watch down upon you."

He nodded at her puzzled expression. “Aye. Don’t think your companions at the *Kraken’s Curse* will escape their wrath. Nor, I’m afraid, will the less fortunate benefit from the fallout.”

She glared hard at the old man who looked calmly back at her. Rage seethed behind her eyes. Not trusting herself to speak, she turned and opened the balcony door; disappearing into the misty darkness.

Thoril’s words followed her into the night. “By delivering the Crusher Scroll, you’re sealing the fate of the kingdom.”

Larina

All Great Stories Must End

Lichen beneath Larina's grasping fingers made scaling the perimeter wall of the Banebridge Manor estate impossible. After dropping silently to the lawn, she kept her eyes on the return of several guards as they casually made their way back to the manor; oblivious to what had just transpired inside. Now that she had reached the wall, the truth of her original misgivings about the barrier were proving true. The flat surface, encrusted with wet lichen, wasn't conducive to climbing.

There were seven guards in total; five men and two women. Slinking from shadow to shadow, she zipped across the lawn undetected by those employed to keep people like her out. She grimaced. They hadn't kept her out, but the obstacle before her prevented her from leaving.

She sprinted along the base of the wall searching for a way to get over it—a crack in the stone, a statue erected close to the wall, a nearby tree or even a bush—something to give her that extra support she needed to reach the top of the wall.

Several times, she ran at the wall—jumping high and scrambling. More than once her fingertips flashed along the lip but she couldn't hang on.

She passed by the back of the manor, its bulk a blotch of darkness in the fog. If she didn't find a way out soon, she would arrive at the main gate. The black iron entry would be much easier to scale, but it was too well guarded. She'd never make it over before they took her down.

The eastern perimeter showed no signs of being any better than the western or northern stretches. As she slipped by the front of the manor off to her right, she dove behind a dragon statue several paces away from the base of the wall and listened. Doors were banging in the night and raised voices called out to one another. The guards had been alerted to the theft.

Sweat beaded on her forehead and soaked the inside of her leather clothing despite the cold, night air. It wouldn't be long before they found her.

Shouts sounded all over the grounds—most of the voices a long way off. She could only imagine that they were tracing her progress across the damp lawn. She hadn't taken any steps to conceal her passage so it wouldn't be hard for a decent tracker to follow her route.

Discarding any hope of remaining hidden, she bolted along the eastern wall and rounded the southern face. The taller gate posts appeared through the mist up ahead. Standing on the inside of the iron barriers, four guards wandered down the main walkway toward the manor—their attention drawn by the commotion of their peers.

Larina wasted no time taking advantage of their lapse of vigilance. Keeping the wall at her back, she approached the gate without a sound. Thick, black poles and heavy iron cross braces comprised the bulk of the gateway. Swirling curves surrounded large, iron, dragon faces in the centre of each gate.

Though slick in her grasp due to the heavy moisture in the air, her leather gloves gave her sufficient purchase to pull her slight frame up the inside of the barrier—her weight not enough to rattle the massive enclosure.

It wasn't until she was near the top that she spotted four more guards milling about on the roadway beyond. Their attention seemed to lie on something she couldn't see.

Getting over the spiked tops of the metal uprights proved challenging. One slip and she would impale herself on the sharp tips. She grasped two spikes by their ends and physically lifted her body over the top. Once clear, she pushed off and vaulted to the ground; landing in a crouch.

One of the guards on the road turned at the faint sound of her feet hitting the ground. "There!"

All seven guards—three outside and four inside the gate—spun to catch sight of what the first guard pointed at. A young woman clad entirely in black except for the tan, snakeskin thongs she used to keep her ankle-length breeks tight around her boots, rose up from the ground with a dagger in hand.

Before any of the guards outside the gate could react, she sprinted out wide and was beyond them; jumping high into the air to miss being struck by a hastily thrown polearm.

She angled her course to a different street than the one she had travelled on her way to the top of the fjord. Fleet as a cat, her swift footfalls carried her away from Banebridge Manor—each long stride creating distance between herself and her pursuers.

Clad in heavy armour and bearing many weapons, the guards had no chance of keeping up.

Soaked with sweat and exhausted, Larina searched the façade of the old administrative building from the safety of an alley across the street, half a block away.

Larina

Besides the usual bodies slunk in dark places that most people wouldn't think of searching, and a cat sniffing at something in the middle of the rain washed, cobblestone street descending the side of the fjord just beyond the building she watched, nothing stirred.

She estimated by the moon's position as it dropped behind the lofty peaks of the western mountains flanking the water far below that dawn wasn't far-off. The *Kraken's Curse* never closed, but before she rendezvoused with Korwynn, she had to check on Allard.

The damp cobblestones beneath her feet grounded her emotions. She could feel every seam and nuance in their texture as she padded softly down the deserted street.

The animal she thought was a cat rose onto its hind legs; lifting its pointed nose and sniffing at the air—beady red eyes watching her approach.

Larina gave the feral rat a wide berth. Aware of the diseases vermin carried, she feared them more than the Watch.

She stopped beside the gaping doorway of the administrative building and listened. Nothing. She wasn't sure if that was a good thing or not. Bear had promised to come straight here and move Allard and anyone else who might have fallen afoul of the Watch because of her transgressions.

She cast a quick look around the street before slipping into the large foyer and bounding noiselessly up the right stairwell. Her distracted gaze registered the markings of what appeared to be heavy traffic that had disturbed the dust and debris around the broken fountain; the tracks visible in the moonlight filtering through grimy windows along the west facing wall.

Larina

The condition of the second-floor landing filled her with dread. Most of the doorways remained undisturbed—broken and filled with collapsed stone and fallen walls—but it was the few doorways that had been covered in tatty sheets that made her stare open-mouthed. They lay in crumpled heaps, scattered and torn amongst debris on the landing.

Without having to enter the rooms, she already knew what had happened. The smell of death hung in the stale air. The iron tang of spilled blood and the strong aroma of feces and urine turned up her nose.

A quick search of the closest room confirmed her worst fear. Two older men and a woman of indeterminable age lay in a pool of blood, their vacant stares mocking her. She was too late.

Taking the stairs two at a time, she noticed blood stains on the steps. She wasn't positive, but she didn't think the smears had been there before.

As the steps passed excruciatingly slow beneath her, she couldn't help wonder what had happened to Bear. Would she find him among the dead? Her stomach rose to her throat, constricting her ability to breathe.

She slipped in a fresh puddle of blood at the top of the stairwell as she charged into the room overlooking the fjord. Sliding to a halt within the doorway, her worst nightmare stared her in the face. Allard lay on the blood-splattered floor, his legs bent beneath him at unnatural angles. A dark stain radiated from beneath withered hands cupping his waist. In the back corner, the remains of a younger man lay butchered beneath the pile of old rags. A quick look confirmed it wasn't Bear.

She dropped to her knees and grabbed Allard by his frail shoulders and shook him—her vision clouded by tears running freely down her cheeks.

Larina

"Allard." Her voice broke as his head lolled on his neck.

She looked around the room, desperately needing someone to comfort her, but she was alone.

Hugging the old knight to her chest, she rocked his lifeless body back and forth like a mother soothing a newborn babe. Wracked by heavy sobs, she found it hard breathe. She half spit as her hoarse voice softly escaped her trembling lips, "Rest well, my sweet prince. May you find peace in your princess' arms."

Early morning light shooed the darkness from the room. The sky visible beyond the large, panelled windows, was a beautiful light blue. Any sign of the previous day's storm, long since forgotten.

Larina opened weary eyes, hoping it had all been a bad dream. Allard's waxen face told her otherwise. She stared at him through misty eyes, and ran a shaking fingertip over his unshaven face.

She tried to console herself. At least he was at peace now. No more fighting for survival in rat infested alleyways; shivering away what little body heat his bony frame could muster.

She stared numbly at his lifeless form for a long time, unable to come to terms with how badly she had failed him. Vulnerable and unable to look after himself, this once mighty warrior's death had been the direct result of her bad decision. If she had only kept her outrage in check and not visited the watchtower, perhaps the old knight would still be alive.

Her eyes flicked to the unknown man in the corner. She had failed them both.

She sighed and sat up to adjust her tunic. The suede tube jabbed into her side. Pulling it free, she resisted the urge to crumple it in her hands. If the strangers hadn't forced her into doing their dirty work a day early, she would have been here to defend Allard.

She threw the tube against the wall, not caring if it damaged the cursed artifact. It bounced and rolled into the middle of the room, coming to rest by a pile of Allard's new clothing. Her tears started again. What good were the clothes now?

She swallowed past the lump that wouldn't leave her throat and observed the room in the morning light. Much of the broken furniture looked worse off than it had before. Food from the bucket she had brought lay scattered and destroyed from the passage of boots. Blood stains on the wall and splattered on a few of the windowpanes bespoke of a great fight.

She smiled through her grief. Sir Allard hadn't gone down quietly.

Wiping her face on one of Allard's new blankets, she dabbed at her eyes until she could see clearly again. She smiled with a broken heart at one of the only people who had ever truly cared about her. She envisioned how handsome he must've been in his youth.

With the greatest of care, she pulled a few wisps of straggly hair from the corners of his face and lovingly shaved his whiskers. Sir Allard always liked a clean face.

Thankful for the keen edge of her dagger, her thoughts drifted to her other true friend. Why hadn't Bear been here? He had promised. The pain of his betrayal twisted her empty stomach to the point that she thought she might vomit.

After changing Allard's blood-soaked shirt into something more befitting a royal knight, she laid him out in a dignified position with his hands clasped together over his stomach. She wished she had a sword to place in his grasp. She briefly entertained placing her dagger in his hands, but thought better of it. She was going to need it real soon.

As she moved his left hand, she noticed a wad of paper crumpled within his fingers. She pried it free and opened the blood-stained note. Written by a shaky hand were the words:

The hour is dark. Judging by the what I hear happening on the floor below, I fear my time has come. Do not mourn for me. I have lived a wonderful life.
All great stories must end. I've already taken the stage. My part in the play is over. It's your turn, my dear Larina. Enjoy life for all it's worth. Leave this infernal place and do me proud.
Forever your knight in waiting,
Sir Allard

She struggled to read the entire note; fighting to see beyond the tears blinding her. Her gaze took in the room, searching for the quill he had used. Beneath the windowsill, propped between a fallen piece of the exterior wall rock, she located a tiny inkpot with a stained cap and a feathered quill that had seen better days. Stamped on the inkpot's cap was the sigil of King Peter Svelte, the Warrior: an eagle with wings poised for landing, clutching a sword in its talons.

She held the note to her chest and wept. When the tears came no more, she wiped her face and blew her nose on a blanket she had bought for him.

She dressed the unknown man in a new tunic and laid him out peacefully beside Allard. With a heavy sigh, she stared vacantly through the grimy window at the tranquil bay far below. If she lived through what she was about to undertake, she would return and see that Allard and the rest of the unfortunate victims of Danth Emerald's vengeance were interred in the moors overlooking the fjord.

Larina

The Warrior

Thunderhead Fjord glistened beneath the midmorning sun cresting the eastern peaks of The Spine. Larina stared at the calm water from a vantage point three tiers above the shoreline. The peaceful bay belied the chaos that she was about to perpetrate on Storms End.

Keeping to the alleyways as much as possible, she made her way toward the *Kraken's Curse*. She had no idea how she was going to react to Korwynn and his lackeys when she confronted them, but if they gave her trouble over her compensation, she swore to slit their throats and spit on their corpses.

A distinct aroma of acrid smoke turned up her nostrils—the top of the blackened watchtower visible from where she stood. A sad smile crossed her face. Had it not gone so badly…

Anger simmered in her chest. The time for crying was done. It was time for retribution. Time to do what shc should have done long ago. End the vile reign of the Watch captain, Danth Emerald. He would die on the end of her dagger if it took her dying breath.

The citizens passing her on the street cast her a strange look—many giving her a wide berth. Though used to such treatment, she couldn't recall people reacting *that* strongly to her presence. Perhaps word had filtered down to street level that the baron had decided to come down hard on the Storms End Lightning Bolt.

She eyed the blade clutched firmly in her hand and raised her eyebrows. It could be the dagger.

Whatever. With the murder of Allard, she had stopped caring. She stepped toward three men who were walking together and gawking at her; brandishing her knife. "What're you looking at?"

Their eyes grew wide as they jumped out of the way.

"Easy lady. No need to get violent," the biggest man said, but that was as far as he took the argument.

Larina ignored him and strutted brazenly down the last set of steep hills. If the Watch were looking for her, let them come.

The smell of smoke grew strangely stronger the closer she got to a bridge leading over the aqueduct to Canal Road. Most of the people in the lower tiers were huddled in groups, talking and pointing at something beyond the centre of the lower city.

She followed their gazes, not seeing anything at first but the flight of a strangely familiar bird. During a lull in the stiff breeze blowing off the bay, she noticed a plume of black smoke waft above the taller buildings beyond the city centre. Something else was burning.

'Good,' she thought.

The pungent smoke filled her with bittersweet emotions. There was nothing to be done about the watchtower now, but oh, how amazing it had felt to watch it burn. It was time for payback. If anything, the new fire would keep curious eyes off her movements until she collected her reward and started after her prey.

Larina

The more she thought about it, the more she debated whether or not to inspect whatever it was that was on fire. The Watch would be present.

She slowed her pace. Though she didn't care what happened to her, she wasn't naïve. If she came upon the Watch and Danth wasn't present, she might lose her chance to end him.

She skirted across Canal Road and slipped behind a large warehouse fronting the bay—opting to walk along the waterfront away from the street.

Dock hands and warehouse workers went about their duties, ignoring her for the most part. A few turned their heads her way but no one tried to confront her. Amongst the rough and tumble dock hands, she was just another hardy soul going about her business.

Snippets of conversation reached her ears as she went.

"A real shame that…"

"Need to be finding another hole in the wall…"

"Wonder who they're after…?"

"Did you hear about the one they call the Rock…?"

Larina stopped and spun on the burly, bare-chested brute standing at the head of a pier and speaking with another similarly unclad male. Stepping between them, she placed her dagger under the speaker's chin and snarled, "What about the Rock?"

"Hey!" The man tried to step back and almost fell off the dock.

The second man raised a hand to disarm her, but she ducked and came up behind him—the dagger pricking the base of his spine.

"Whoa, lady?" the second man yelped, raising large, dirty hands into the air.

"Geez, missus. Have you gone mad? What have we done to you?" The first dock worker asked, his deep-set eyes searching the immediate area for assistance.

Larina didn't dignify him with an answer. She pressed the dagger into the other man's back—its razor-sharp blade drawing blood. "I said, what about the Rock?"

The victim's wild eyes glared at his companion for help; his face knotted in pain.

The first man blurted, "They killed him."

The shock of those three simple words sucked the fight from her. She released her victim and stumbled backward as the ramifications of the Master of Storms End's warning struck home. *'The watchtower incident will provoke the baron into bringing the full weight of the Watch down upon you...Don't think your companions at the Kraken's Curse will escape their wrath.'*

Not caring about the two sailors who were pulling large filleting knives from leather sheaths at their waists, Larina sprinted along the shoreline. Twice, she pushed a worker out of her path as she stormed by, knocking one man into the harbour, and upsetting a pile of straw baskets the other carried. The irate dock hands fell far behind and gave up the chase.

As she rounded the corner of a fishery and bolted up the alley separating it from another warehouse, her footfalls slowed to a staggering halt. Across Canal Road, beyond a crowd of onlookers, blackened rafters resembling charred ribs protruded above the stone walls of what had been the *Kraken's Curse*.

Her dagger forgotten, it almost slipped from her hand. To her horror, she watched a group of soot-stained citizens drag an unrecognizable body from the ruins while another group slowly handed buckets back and forth from the canal.

Larína

A stiff breeze blew off the bay, ruffling her unkempt hair around her dirt-smeared face. How long she stood there in total disbelief, she had no idea, but sensing someone behind her, she whirled around and slashed with her dagger—expecting to cut one of the dock workers she had offended.

Draped in a pale, deer hide tunic adorned with frills hanging from the elbows and lining the out seams of a pair of matching leggings, a darker-skinned woman held palms out, signifying she meant Larina no harm.

Larina stared hard at the beautiful woman with glistening black hair that fell beyond her waist—bound behind her head with a woven, leather headband. A single eagle feather adorned the back of the headband and protruded above the woman's head. The same female archer that had chased her across the rooftops.

"Stay back."

"I won't hurt you," the woman said with an unfamiliar accent.

Larina found that hard to believe. The woman had come close to hitting her during their chase the other night.

An unstrung bow protruded over the woman's right shoulder; the fletches of many arrows peeked above her left.

"Not hurt me? You tried to kill me." Larina contemplated her options.

The woman raised thick, black eyebrows. "If Lozen try to kill, Lozen would kill."

Larina swallowed. The woman didn't appear dangerous at the moment, and yet, she knew instinctively that Lozen had followed her here.

"Come with me."

"Ha. I'm not going anywhere with you." Larina started to back away. She glanced at the crowd gathered around the *Kraken*. No one appeared to be looking her way. She turned and dashed across the narrow street, searching for Danth Emerald.

He wasn't amongst the Watch gathered there, but her breath caught as she locked eyes with Fren.

His startled gaze lit up—his face red with recent burns. Tattered hair and scorched eyebrows attested to the fact that he had barely escaped the watchtower inferno. "There's the Bolt! Grab her!"

Larina stumbled. She looked every which way at once. The city guard jumped into action, filling the roadway on either side.

Unable to run down Canal Road, and unwilling to return to the alley where Lozen was emerging with her bow strung, Larina ran past the crowd to the spot where Rock liked to stand next to the canal. Lengthening her stride, she bounded through the air, leaping high over the waterway. She knew before her feet left the ground that there was no way she was could vault its entire width.

Intakes of wondrous gasps followed her progress over the putrid water.

Her flight fell short. She broke the surface with a great splash, but her arms and legs never stopped moving. She was up and out the other side faster than anyone could react.

"Get her!" Fren hollered, his scarred face shaking with fury.

The city folk stared dumbly after her; the heavily armoured guards balked at jumping into the canal.

"She's getting away, you fools!" Spit flew from Fren's lips.

Larina looked away but Fren's next words weren't lost on her.

"Ah! The Warrior! Take her!"

Larina

An arrow shattered against the stone lip of the canal at Larina's feet. Sparing a glance across the waterway, Lozen stood in the middle of Canal Road with another arrow nocked.

Larina searched the building she stood behind for the nearest alleyway to run into.

A heart-stopping whistle of an arrow flew by her ear and embedded itself in the wooden wall of the building with a twang.

She stared wide-eyed. Lozen advanced to the edge of the canal, calmly pulling a third arrow from her quiver.

Not wishing to test fate, Larina turned to run but a grisly sight stopped her in her tracks.

A bloated white corpse floated in the water—an arrow buried between its eyes.

Stunned, Larina almost stumbled into the canal. Rock's vacant stare mocked her from just below the surface.

An arrow whacked against the wall behind her, exploding into a shower of splinters. With a last look at the devilish archer, Larina fled headlong up a narrow alleyway and out of harm's way.

Fren's frantic shouts could be heard well after she crossed the next roadway and started up the steep street beyond.

Larina

Gom

Larina's thighs screamed as she rounded a street corner on the fourth tier and bent over to catch her breath. She couldn't get the image of Rock's dead eyes from her head. It was as if he stared at her from beyond the grave—accusing her for his, and everyone else associated with the *Kraken's Curse*, death.

Nor could she forget the savage stare of the woman who called herself Lozen. She had never seen such an exquisite-looking female before. Darker-skinned, round cheeks, and intelligent brown eyes shrouded beneath heavy brows; all surrounded by the blackest hair she had ever seen. The intensity of the woman's demeanor had unsettled her almost as much as her chilling words, *'If Lozen try to kill, Lozen would kill.'*

All of her earlier bravado had been sapped from her at the sight of the *Kraken's Curse,* but seeing Rock, lifeless in the canal, left her numb.

Thoril Banebridge hadn't been kidding when he said the baron would come down on her with the full weight of the Watch. She couldn't believe that the leader of Storms End would order the execution of people whose only tie to her was the fact they frequented the same tavern.

She held her hands in front of her, unable to stop them from shaking. First, a cowardly attack on Allard and the rest of the downtrodden residents in the old administrative building, and now, the *Kraken's Curse*. Bearing witness to the senseless destruction, her gut told her what she didn't want to hear. The Watch had declared war on everyone she had ever involved herself with.

Her mind spun out of control, making it difficult to focus on her surroundings. Her gaze flew from one spot on the street to another; imagining all of the places someone might be hiding and watching her.

She ducked into a crouch, cowering. In her mind, the vision of the Warrior inhabited all of those places. Everywhere she turned, the archer stared back at her with those haunting brown eyes; sighting an arrow she held drawn.

Arms wrapped tightly about her to fend off a deeper cold than the morning air, her thoughts turned to Bear. She admonished herself for her earlier misgivings about her best friend. Her only friend. Bear would never betray her trust. He would do anything she asked. If he said he was going to help Allard escape, that's what he would have set out to do. Bear was a sensible man, but she knew in her heart that when it came to her, he would put aside his reservations and do whatever it took to make her happy. Even if that led to his death.

She reached out and latched onto the corner of the wooden building; pulling herself upright. Trembling from head to foot, she swallowed past the lump in her throat. If Bear hadn't made it to the old administrative building, that only meant one thing. Something had happened to him.

The large bells of the Storms End temple sounded eerily from the city centre—their hollow clangs echoing off the towering fjord walls.

Drawn to the clamour, Larina stepped free of the alley and followed the curious stares of the people on the roadway.

Larina

A black warship sailed down the fjord toward the harbour; three tall masts boasting full sails beneath a flag embroidered with the sigil of Storms End: a great silver warhammer striking a green serpent on a black background. Before Helleden's attack two years ago, Storms End boasted the third largest fleet in all of Zephyr. Only the great cities of Apexceal, far to the south, and Madrigail Bay had more boats conscripted by the king.

After the sorcerer's campaign, Zephyr's northern fleet had been wiped out. Storms End had only been able to build three ships in the aftermath, and Larina could see two of them at anchor near the southern watchtower.

With any luck, the arrival of the ship would further distract the Watch and allow her to discover where Korwynn had gone to ground. She was surprised she hadn't been contacted by him or his men yet, but with the destruction of the *Kraken's Curse*, it made sense.

She wanted to be rid of the troublesome scroll and come to terms with what she was going to do next. Killing Danth was her main objective, but after witnessing the retaliation from the Watch, the captain's demise might be better thought out than just a head on attack.

First, she needed to find Bear. A prospect she wasn't looking forward to. If something had happened to her dearest friend, she wasn't sure what she would do.

Ensuring no one other than curious bystanders were aware of her presence at the end of the alley, she checked her dagger was secure and shuffled into the open, remaining close to the buildings on the near side of the winding road, and keeping her head down.

She watched the movement of the citizens through the long hair cascading over her face as she made her way toward a building she had been sworn never to return to. Bear's house.

Larina

Never married, Bear lived with his parents. She liked to tease him about it, but he always shrugged it off—claiming that one day all his saved-up coin would buy him a manor at the top of the fjord.

It was on Bear's insistence that she never seek him out at his parent's house—not wishing to draw unfavourable attention to them. The type of attention Larina's activities were likely to attract. It had been a delicate conversation, but she understood.

Given the current situation, she felt she had no choice. As long as she was careful, what harm could come of a quick visit to confirm her friend was safe?

The fifth tier marked the division between the more affluent citizens of the lower city and those whose life hadn't been so kind. Bear's parents owned one of the minor mercantiles on the third tier—known by most as the market.

To be sure she wasn't being followed, Larina spent time walking up and down alleyways. When she was within sight of the stone rowhouse she was looking for, she doubled back and waited.

Dogs barked and doors banged. Voices came and went, but no one struck her as suspicious. Ever so carefully, she strolled across the road and slipped behind the rowhouse.

Bear's residence was the third of six. Hopping a decorative picket fence hemming in a tiny plot of vegetables, she rapped on the weathered backdoor.

It took two more tries before a stooped, grey-haired woman answered—opening the door and leaning close to study Larina's face. "Yes?"

"Hi ma'am. It's me." Larina cast a furtive glance up and down the thin line of backyards. An unscalable rock shelf rose up to the sixth tier beyond a narrow path that ran behind the fenced yards.

The woman squinted but it was obvious she didn't recognize Larina. "What would you like, then?"

Larina wasn't sure whether she should be hurt or thankful that Bear's mother had forgotten her. "Is B..." She caught herself. Bear was his street name—one she doubted he had told his parents about. "Is Gom home?"

The woman's wrinkled visage twisted into an ugly sneer. "We don't want none." She hocked and spat at Larina's feet and slammed the door in her face.

Shocked, Larina blinked at the door, wondering what she had said to deserve that. Had Bear's mother recognized her after all? Feeling helpless, she looked along the back of the long building. Thankfully, no one was outside.

She stared at the door a while longer, debating whether to knock again, but decided against it. She started picking her way through the garden, careful not to squish the plants.

The door flew open with a crash. "Oi!" A deep, male voice shouted. "What're you doing traipsing around the gardens?"

Larina turned to see Bear's father. The balding man resembled a much older Bear—aged, baggy skin hanging on a large frame bent with age. Loose clothing that had properly fit him once upon a time hung off his body like worn, wrinkled sheets. Unlike Bear's mother, his mannerism spoke of someone who still retained his senses.

"Hi, Mr. Haulkins. Remember me?"

The large man closed the door behind him and stepped into the garden—no footwear on his dirty feet. He squinted and tilted his head; scratching his scalp until recognition softened his features for a moment before contorting into vexation. "You're that trollop that's gotten our Gom into a heap of trouble. You got nerve showing your face around here."

Larina gaped at his response. "Wha—"

"Get yourself away from here. Me and the missus don't need no trouble."

"I don't know what you're talking about."

"You're the one that set fire to the watchtower, ain'tcha?"

The Haulkins had been good to her after her mother had died. They had given her a roof over her head on a few occasions; preventing her from starving as a child. She attributed a lot of her character to how charitable and giving they had been to her. Though she hadn't seen them in years, she was shocked by how time had ravaged the kindly couple.

She couldn't lie to him. "Aye, but there's a reason for that. I didn't mean to—"

"Didn't mean to? Hah! What? You just happened to set a stone building on fire? One owned by the Watch?"

She had a hard time holding his scathing glare. Swallowing her discomfort, she stared at the ground. "That wasn't my idea, trust me. If you knew of the grief it's caused me since, you—"

"Grief it's caused you?" Mr. Haulkins voice was incredulous. "Did you see me missus? Gom's incarceration has addled her brain! Haven't you caused us enough grief?"

"Wait. What? Gom's been taken by the Watch?"

"Dragged out of a building in the upper tiers last night. Accused of aiding a felon. Rumour has it, the baron plans to make an example out of him." His accusatory glare shrivelled her heart. "First Cassie, and now Gom. Why won't you leave us alone?"

The insinuation that she had been responsible for Cassie's death stunned her. She had often wondered why the Haulkins attitude toward her had changed after her best friend was found dead, but she never believed they thought the unfortunate event had anything to do with her. She swallowed. She had trouble believing it wasn't her fault either.

Not knowing what to say, she turned and left the garden with slumped shoulders.

"You best never come back, you hear? Next time I see you, I'll drag you to the Watch myself."

Mr. Haulkins words bit into her—each one twisting the dagger he had driven into her heart.

Larina

Not the Indian Way

It had almost killed her to return to the old administrative building to fetch one of the hooded tunics she had bought for the less fortunate citizens of Storms End, but if she wished to keep her identity hidden from those who were actively searching for her, she needed to hide her appearance.

She contemplated shaving her head with her dagger but decided it would take too much time. Rumours gathered from bits of conversation she had overheard on the way to the administrative building spoke of a public execution being arranged for the middle of the afternoon. One that was aimed at setting an example for anyone who might be withholding information regarding her whereabouts. Though no names were mentioned, she had a sinking premonition that Bear was the example.

She hurried from the building and made her way down to the wide commons in the heart of the first tier; keeping to the alleys and backstreets as much as possible.

Sitting with her back against the corner of an ancient temple that had survived both of Helleden's invasions and several Kraidic attempts at sacking the city, she tucked her hair inside her brown hooded tunic; head bowed low to avoid detection.

Several members of the Watch formed a perimeter around the gallows' structure dominating the city centre. Perched atop one of the hanging arms, a falcon turned its head back and forth in quick jerks, as if watching for something. The same bird she had seen along the docks before she had come across the destruction of the *Kraken's Curse*.

She stared at the sleek falcon as she dreamed of better days. As children, she and Cassie used to clamber all over the heinous structure; pretending to be executioners on some occasions, and the ones scheduled to hang on others. One time, Bear had come across them and allowed them to escort him solemnly up the flight of steps along the back side of the platform and place one of the scratchy ropes around his neck. She shook her head at the irony.

Her stomach grumbled continuously, but she didn't care. She wasn't hungry.

Scenario after scenario went through her mind on how she might disrupt the proceedings if Bear *was* the one to be executed. Looking past her lowered brow at the disciplined, well-armed Watch, none of those scenarios were likely to end well.

The stench of the canal wafted up the alley to where she sat. The aqueduct curved around the wide area comprising the city centre, sluggishly flowing behind the cavernous temple. Several bridges built close to one another spanned the waterway, connecting the many roads that descended from the upper tiers to the commons.

Every time a new person entered the expansive grounds, she tracked them until she was convinced they weren't searching for her.

So enrapt in her observation of the gathering crowd, she almost screamed when a hand grasped the top of her shoulder and prevented her from moving.

Lozen's intelligent, brown eyes stared down at her.

Larina reached for her dagger and tried to extricate herself, but Lozen's iron grip held fast. The sight of Lozen's thick-bladed knife, its serrated edge held close to her face, stopped her hand.

The woman subtly shook her head in warning. "I won't hurt you."

Larina's eyes crossed staring at the tip of Lozen's blade, finding it hard to believe the woman's claim.

"Master Banebridge sent me."

Larina frowned, her gaze finding an odd warmth in the strange woman's eyes. "Why would he do that?"

"He's looking for fighters."

"Huh?" Lozen wasn't making sense. If Thoril was recruiting people, Larina was certain she was the *last* person he wished to enlist. "Do you even know who I am?"

Lozen lowered her knife and eased her grip. "You're the one they call the Bolt."

Larina took the opportunity to spring to her feet. Not wishing to draw attention to herself, she side-stepped Lozen and moved deeper into the alley; her gaze noting the woman's unstrung bow strapped across her back.

Until she knew whether Bear was the subject of the gathering, she had to resist the urge to bolt down the alley and flee. A sinking feeling told her that even if she did, she wouldn't lose the exotic woman this time. Resisting the urge to pull her dagger, she asked, "Old man Banebridge wants fighters for what?"

Lozen tilted her head. "Old man?"

"You said, Master Banebridge."

"Master Banebridge isn't old."

"Not old? I don't know where you're from, but in Zephyr, Master Banebridge is *old*."

Lozen slipped her dagger into the sheath she wore hidden at the small of her back. "I'm a warrior of the Elk Tribe. Our land is high in the Altirius Mountains."

Lozen's words meant nothing to Larina. "Didn't Master Banebridge tell you what I did last night?"

Lozen's heavy brow came together. She shook her head. "You spoke to Master Banebridge?"

Larina nodded. Lozen's surprise made sense. If she knew about Larina's treachery, she would have slit her throat instead of greeting her with a hand on the shoulder. "Let's just say we had a heart-to-heart talk early this morning. As a result of that conversation, I must respectfully decline your invitation."

"You're a mysterious woman, Bolt. How could you talk to Master Banebridge?" She took a step backward. "Are you a witch?"

"Hah! Not likely. Been called worse, though."

"I'm not understanding. Master Banebridge just sailed in." Lozen stepped to the edge of the alley and pointed at the three black galleons visible beyond a break in the waterfront.

Totally captivated by the bizarre conversation, Larina stepped in behind Lozen and peered over her shoulder at the black warships she indicated. A fleeting thought of taking advantage of Lozen's vulnerability crossed her mind, but something about the woman stayed her hand. Instead, she said quietly, "Master Banebridge can't be on that ship. I just left him this morning."

Lozen leaned her head out to the side so she could gaze into Larina's puzzled eyes. "You were with Pollard this morning?"

Larina backed up a step. "Pollard?"

"Who do you think…?" Lozen followed her into the alley, a slight smile tuning up her lips. "Ah. We're not speaking of the same Master. You spoke with Thoril."

Larina's eyes widened as the mystery unravelled. Lozen meant Thoril's fully grown son. The man that Bear used to hang around with. She corrected herself—the giant that Bear claimed made Tiny look small.

Conflicting emotions tore at Larina. She couldn't abandon Bear and yet, though she had never met the man, she knew of Pollard. If the son of Thoril had returned on the baron's request to capture her…Or worse. If Pollard had been summoned by the Master of the council because of the Crusher Scroll…

Larina's frown deepened. That didn't make sense. She had just stolen it. "I need to get out of here."

"No. You must wait for Master Banebridge. He's looking for you."

Larina nodded and took a couple of steps to create distance between them. "Exactly."

She started running toward the canal, not looking forward to another swim, but Lozen's voice froze her.

"Hold!"

Larina waited for the arrow to bury itself in her back. When it didn't come, she glanced over her shoulder. Lozen walked casually down the alley, palms held out to show she wasn't a threat.

"Pollard will protect you from the Watch."

Larina turned, her hand on the hilt of her dagger. "Protect me?"

"The Watch is hunting you. Captain Emerald wants you dead. Pollard wants you alive."

Larina frowned. Nothing Lozen said made sense. She remembered the archer chasing her across the rooftops, and again outside the *Kraken's Curse* this morning—both times shooting arrows at her. "You're lying. You tried to kill me. You're working with the Watch. They hired you to bring me in."

Lozen nodded as if confirming Larina's accusation, but her calm words contradicted the action. "That is not the Indian way."

Lozen reached behind her back.

Larina's dagger flew into her hand.

Lozen's did likewise. As well as her unstrung bow. She held them out for Larina to see. Curiously, she laid them at her feet. Nodding to Larina, she backed away from her weapons. "You see? Lozen doesn't want to hurt you. If Lozen wanted to kill, Lozen would kill."

"But…" Larina checked behind her, expecting to see Danth Emerald, but no one else was in the alley. "I don't understand. That was you with the Watch the other night. You fired arrows at me. And again, this morning."

Lozen's smile lifted her pudgy cheeks. "No. Lozen made a trick. Lozen missed. If Lozen wanted to, Lozen wouldn't miss." She wagged a long, slender finger and indicated her abandoned weapons with a nod. "Lozen is an honourable warrior. You must trust Lozen."

A roar from the commons interrupted their tense stand-off. They looked beyond the shadowy alleyway to the large platform erected in the middle of the city square.

Forgetting about Lozen, Larina charged past her and stopped at the front corner of the towering, stone temple. She pulled her cowl tight around her face and ducked low. The crowd's collective gaze appeared to stare straight at her.

A bell clanged somewhere overhead. She looked up, past an enormous, sprawling stonework that depicted a two-masted ship riding heavy seas—a kraken wrapped about its keel and a trio of dragons diving out of roiling clouds overhead. Several men draped in religious robes exited the vaulted double doors of the temple and formed a line on either side of a wide, white marble platform that led away from the temple to a broad set of steps that curved out to encompass the width of the impressive building.

The Bishop of Storms End, his head topped with a light-blue, conical cap, led a procession of Storms End Watch. He held a long-handled bell in front of him, ringing it in practiced cadence.

Larina had forgotten the bishop's name it had been so long since she had attended a sermon, but the sight of the scruffy bearded man stumbling along behind made her gasp.

Bruised and battered, hands restrained in irons that were joined by a rattling chain to a set of heavy manacles secured around his ankles, Bear struggled to shuffle after the clergyman.

Four members of the Watch walked closely behind, unceremoniously shoving Bear forward and catching him by his ripped and filthy tunic whenever he stumbled to his knees. Bringing up the rear of the procession, partially obscured beside the overweight baron, Danth Emerald proudly kept pace.

All reason left Larina in a wild surge of rage.

Larina

Don't You Dare Look Her in the Eye

"**Bolt,**" Lozen whispered harshly and reached out to grab Larina. "No!"

Larina evaded her grasp and clambered up the back of the stonework like a mountain lion springing to the attack. Slipping behind the stern of the ship and vaulting to the sculpted, granite balustrade, she threw her legs over the railing and landed beside the baron with her dagger drawn.

The baron cried out in surprise; his voice changing as Larina's blade glanced off a rib below his shoulder blade and slid into his back. "That's for ordering the slaughter."

The baron dropped to his side, howling in pain.

The dagger had no sooner bit into the baron than Larina pulled it free. She lunged at Danth Emerald.

The captain of the Watch stumbled sideways, preventing the swiping knifepoint from slicing his neck.

"Assassin!" Danth shouted and attempted to draw his sword.

Larina never missed a step. She turned and drove her shoulder under Danth's chin. Her momentum lifted his feet off the ground and slammed his lower back onto the opposing railing with brutal force.

Wrapped in each other's arms, they toppled over the balustrade and fell into a trough between the crashing waves of the mirror-image stonework sculpted between the sweeping steps and the far corner of the temple.

Danth landed beside Larina in a heap; his ceremonial tunic entwined with her hooded cloak. He rose to his knees and pulled back a fist, but his punch never came.

A gasp of disbelief escaped his throat. And then another, and finally, a third. His lifeless body fell to its side.

Larina rolled on top of him; her dagger buried in his neck. “And that’s for Allard, you son-of-a-bitch!”

Men and women dressed in Watch livery leaped from the railing and climbed over the carved rock, surrounding Larina, but the curves and uneven surfaces of the sculpture made it difficult to approach with weapons drawn.

Larina pulled her dagger free and wavered over Danth, her face and cloak splattered with his blood.

“Hold!” a stern, female voice commanded.

All eyes turned to gaze at Lozen balanced on the railing overhead; her soft-soled, buckskin boots resting easily on the narrow surface. She held an arrow half-drawn, its business end pointed at Larina’s chest.

Before Larina could think of a way to escape, a male and female member of the Watch jumped in beside her and forced Larina to drop her dagger to the ground. The female yanked Larina’s hood down and wrapped a fist in her hair. With a violent tug, she growled, “Move,” and shoved her out of the wave trough.

Larina and the female guard stumbled to their knees as they hit the cobblestones paving the commons. Larina tried to break free, but the female jerked her head back with such force, Larina staggered backward with a yelp.

A dagger point jabbed Larina’s side. “Try that again and I’ll gut you.”

Larina

The gathered crowd had drifted over to form a large semi-circle around the front of the temple; snippets of their voices reaching Larina.

"Kill her!"

"Whatcha going to do now?"

"Off with her head!"

"You ain't so fast anymore, are you?"

Lozen dropped from the railing into the wave trough and retrieved Larina's dagger; her strung bow over her shoulder. She forced her way through the wall of guards surrounding Larina, a large knife in hand. "I'll take her from here."

A slight smile lit up Larina's face.

The female guard didn't appear like she wished to give up her prize. "Under whose orders? She killed the baron and Captain Emerald. As a captain of the Watch, I'm taking charge."

Lozen nodded toward the gallows, an evil grin splitting her face. "She will die like Danth wanted. We will avenge his death."

Not waiting for a response, Lozen slipped in behind Larina and held the serrated edge of her blade against Larina's throat; shoving her toward the crowd. "The Storms End Lightning Bolt will strike no more."

The female captain nodded but refused to relinquish her hold. Together they half-dragged, half-pushed Larina through the parting throng of people and mounted the steps leading up the back of the gallows.

"Bolt!"

Halfway up the steps, Larina strained her head to the side to get a glimpse of the friendly voice she knew so well.

Surrounded by his own guards, Bear was being shoved up the steps after her.

"Bear! You're alive!"

The captain pulled on her hair. "No talking."

"What're you doing here?" Bear answered. "I told them you'd fled Storms End."

"Ya, well, I guess they know better now, huh?"

"Afraid so. Hey, I'm sorry. I tried to get to Allard. The Watch was there waiting for me! Is he…?"

"The bastards killed them!" Larina tried to shake free of the captain's excruciating hold on her hair.

Their progress up the steep stairway stopped and fell back a couple of steps before the captain and Lozen got her under control. It felt as if the captain had ripped half of the hair from her head.

"I'm sorry Bear. This is all my fault."

"Bah! I'm my own person. I could've refused."

The captain jumped up to the next step, her clenched fist in Larina's face. "I told you to shut it."

Larina tried to head butt her, but the captain ducked away and twisted her grip—wrenching Larina's head back and to the side.

Larina gritted her teeth; refusing to cry out. She twisted in the captain's grasp and spied Bear's group a few steps behind. "I guess this is goodbye, my friend. It's time I danced with the mistress of death."

She caught the concern on Bear's face before the captain jerked her head hard and made her face the climb.

His response made her smile.

"Don't you dare look her in the eye."

"Never!" Her voice peaked as the captain punched her in the stomach.

"Quiet, rat!"

Larina gave the captain a venomous glare and spat in her face.

Larina

"Why you little—" The captain raised a hand to wipe at the spittle.

Larina head butted her in the face, eliciting a sickening crack.

The captain relinquished her hold on Larina's hair; blood spurting from her broken nose.

Larina dug the sole of her boot against the next step and drove backward, taking her and Lozen into the guards jostling Bear up from behind. Men and women toppled from the open staircase as they crashed to the commons in a heap.

All the way down the steps and hitting the ground amongst a tangle of bodies, Lozen's hold on Larina didn't falter. Somehow, the large knife never cut her neck. Whoever this Lozen person was, she possessed incredible strength.

Lozen manhandled Larina to her feet. No matter how hard Larina squirmed, the woman's grip on her elbow never faltered. Twisting Larina's arm behind her back, Lozen shoved her up the first couple of steps and pressed her lips against Larina's ear. "Stop struggling. You're making this worse than it has to be."

Larina lunged her head, trying to hit the side of Lozen's face but wasn't fast enough.

A fist punched her in the small of the back, dropping her to her knees.

A familiar hand wrapped itself in her hair and lifted her back to her feet; the bloodied face of the captain greeting her pain-laced gaze. "I'm going to trip the latch myself."

Larina tried to form a wad of spit but bent over the captain's fist; taking a punch to the stomach. The captain's knee followed, connecting with Larina's face—almost sending them over the side of the steps. If not for Lozen's steadying hand, they would have fallen hard.

Larina

"Spit on me again and I'll dig your teeth out with a branding iron," the captain growled and yanked her up the steps by the hair.

Unable to catch her breath and physically drained, Larina had no choice but to stagger after her. Fighting unconsciousness, her eyes rolled around; vaguely aware of the cheering crowd packed into the commons. Their boisterous jubilation at her imminent death saddened her. She had done nothing to them…Well, nothing to most of them. The more affluent ones, perhaps.

She had devoted her life to provide for, and tend to, the needs of the less fortunate citizens of Storms End. The same people who had once been friends, or even relatives, of the people gathered to witness her execution. It had never made sense to her how someone could simply abandon another person—the excited crowd a sad example of how far society's morals had fallen.

Through all of the pain and confusion, thoughts of her mother made her smile. On her deathbed, the woman had apologized for not giving Larina anything but false hope.

Reflecting back on her short life, Larina silently thanked the wretched woman. Through a twisted turn of fate, her mother had given her so much more.

Because of the hardships Larina had been forced to overcome to keep from dying, her mother's lack of caring had instilled in Larina a profound sense of empathy and compassion for the people around her. And, in her own mind at least, a better comprehension of what was right and what was horribly wrong. In the end, Larina had come to realize that it was better to fight for what she believed in than to allow the inaction of the masses to dictate how she lived her life.

Larina prided herself on how much she had done for those who were unable to provide for themselves—to make wherever they were forced to live a better place to be. On more occasions than she cared to remember, she had spent her days easing their passage to the next world.

She absently noticed Lozen put her mouth close to the captain's ear, whispering something Larina couldn't hear.

The captain laughed and nodded. "I like the way you think."

Lost in a daze, it dawned on Larina that her captors no longer dragged her up steps. Trying to lift her chin, she opened her eyes and the relevance of where she stood slammed into her. A trap door lay beneath her feet.

Glancing sideways, a loop of thick rope beckoned to her.

It wouldn't be long now.

Larina

The End of the Lightning Bolt

Korwynn's dark glare found Larina as she stood beneath the noose intended for her neck. Held firm by the Watch captain, her hand entangled in Larina's hair; Lozen cranked her arm behind her back—her large blade held to her throat. All Larina could do was stare angrily back at him.

The sight of Korwynn and Tiny in the front row was hard to miss. Their sheer size dwarfed most of the Storms End citizens. Where Cyello had gotten to, she couldn't tell. Nor could she help thinking how she'd like to wipe that malevolent look off Korwynn's face with her dagger.

Beside her, two trap doors down, the Watch had their hands full trying to keep Bear from throwing them off the platform.

Despite her impending demise, she smiled at the only friend she had left in the world. "That's it Bear! Give them…oomph—"

The captain punched her in the stomach and wrenched her head back at the same time, preventing her from doubling over in pain.

"Hand me the noose!" the captain commanded one of the Watch surrounding them.

Larina struggled harder, her foot lashing out at the man who stepped in to grab the noose.

"Hold her!" the captain yelled at Lozen.

Larina

Lozen asserted more pressure on Larina's trapped arm. As much as Larina wanted to fight, the pain was too intense. She stopped resisting Lozen's hold, but she continued to lean one way and then another—making the grisly task as difficult as possible.

The sound of skin smacking skin sounded several times from Bear's direction but the captain's hold on her hair prevented Larina from doing anything but looking straight ahead.

She focused on Korwynn. It was his fault she was in this predicament. *Well, partially*, she conceded. Her actions and choices up to the time she had agreed to work for him had been her own.

Korwynn shrugged, holding his palms upward at his side as if asking, "Well?"

Larina smiled. If nothing else, perhaps she could do one last thing to ease her conscience before she went to meet Allard and Cassie.

She strained against the captain's hold to look her in the eye. "I have a last request."

"Hah! You gave up that privilege when you assassinated Danth and the baron."

"No. Listen! It's important. Trust me." Larina struggled but the captain and Lozen pulled her up short.

"Trust you?" The captain's voice was incredulous. "That'll never happen. Today has been a long time coming. It'll mark the end of the Lightning Bolt."

Through gritted teeth, Larina snarled, "Listen! I stole the Crusher Scroll from Thoril Banebridge. I want you to promise me you'll give it back to him. There are people in the crowd who will kill for it."

Larina

"The Crusher Scroll?" The captain exchanged glances with Lozen. The Indian woman nodded and emitted a peculiar whistle.

The captain frowned at Lozen's bizarre behaviour but her words were directed at Larina. "This had better not be a trick or I'll make sure the fall doesn't break your neck. You hear me?"

Larina nodded the best she could.

Reaching into Larina's tunic, the captain's fingers closed on the scroll. "Hasn't anyone searched her yet?"

Larina frowned. The captain had been the one who had taken her into custody.

"Do you have anything else on you?"

She shook her head. Other than her lock pick and the miniature pouch of lubricant she carried hidden within her tunic, she had nothing else. "Just the scroll."

The captain ripped the suede tube free.

"Easy! You'll destroy the contents."

The captain ignored her. Calling to one of the Watch overseeing the execution, she tossed the scroll through the air. "Commander. Take this."

"What the…?" The commander exclaimed. Holding his hands out to catch it, a feathered missile dropped from the sky and snatched the tube in its claws. Several rapid wingbeats took the falcon beyond the temple.

Larina's heart sank. Looking into the crowd, she caught Korwynn's enraged eyes. Judging by his reaction, he wasn't the one who had employed the bird.

"Tygra! Did you see that?" A familiar voice sounded below the platform. Cyello strode into the open and pointed at her.

Korwynn shook his head in disgust. Muttering something to Cyello, the three men turned and lost themselves in the crowd.

Larina's eyes searched the mass of people for a fourth member of their group, but saw no one that stood out. The name, Tygra, must have been directed at Korwynn. Perhaps it was code for something.

"You. Grab the rope," the captain ordered the man already hanging onto it. "Let's get this done."

Larina forced her head around to see that the other group had cinched their noose around Bear's thick neck. "Be strong, Bear! I'll see you on the other side!"

Etched with fear, tears streamed down Bear's cheeks.

She winked and blew him a kiss, mouthing, *'I love you.'*

"Aw, ain't that sweet." The captain sneered, and nodded at a man standing beside a bank of levers. "Just so you know, as punishment for the watchtower, Lozen suggested that you be allowed to watch your friend die slowly."

Thrashing in her captors' grasp, Larina kept her horror-filled gaze on Bear.

Bear's lips started to form a response when a man known to everyone as the commander of the Watch stepped out from behind Bear and ordered, "Pull!"

The appointed man pulled on a lever.

A loud 'snick' marked the release of the trapdoor. Bear's feet dropped through the gaping hole in the platform beneath him.

Larina screamed. She fought against the captain and Lozen, ignoring the pain they inflicted as Bear thrashed and gurgled on the end of the rope; his body slowly descending through the opening and out of sight to the delight of the crowd.

Larina

The captain jerked Larina back into place and shouted at the man holding the noose. "Get it over her head before she throws us all!" Two more male guards moved in to hold Larina steady.

Lozen put her lips against Larina's ear, her voice eerily deep. "Your turn"

Larina's eyes flicked to catch sight of the dark-skinned face.

Lozen held her angered look; a smirk lifting her full lips.

Though the pressure never let up on the arm Lozen held secure behind her back, a strange, cold metal surface was forced into her palm.

Larina's eyes widened.

Lozen winked.

Without warning, Lozen released Larina's arm. Before anyone knew what had happened, the Indian woman shouldered the man holding the rope. He stumbled and fell to the platform, struggling to keep from rolling off the edge.

Lozen pulled her knife clear of Larina and pushed through the pair of shocked guardsmen who had come to assist. Before they could react, she latched onto the taut rope holding Bear; sawing at the rope with tenacity.

"What's she doing? Stop her!" the captain called after Lozen.

The closest member of the Watch latched onto Lozen's shoulders and attempted to wrest her away from the open hole.

Free of Lozen's hold, Larina spun on the captain. Her dagger in hand, she cracked the captain in the face—its hilt smashing the captain's broken nose into a bloody pulp.

The captain cried out and released Larina's hair to hold her ruined face; leaving her unprepared for the soft-soled boot that drove her beyond the edge of the platform.

Larina

The captain screamed, her arms flailing as she dropped from view. A dull thud marked her impact with the cobblestones below.

Shouts from panicked guards drowned each other out. Swords were drawn and bows raised.

Larina charged after Lozen. She brought the butt end of her dagger down on the guard struggling to pull Lozen away.

Lozen's knife cut through. One hand still hanging onto the rope, she teetered on the verge of falling into the opening but steadied herself. She indicated for Larina to go first.

Larina didn't hesitate. Dropping to her rear, she slid into the gap and dropped to the commons below, barely missing Bear who lay writhing on the cobblestones, gasping for air—unable to loosen the rope due to the manacles around his wrists and ankles.

Lozen fell in behind Larina and dropped into a crouch; bow in hand; an arrow nocked and half drawn. She aimed it at the motionless body of the captain; her intense gaze daring the guards closing in on them to come at her. Three arrows lay at her feet.

Struggling to loosen the noose around Bear's neck, Larina marvelled at how fast Lozen had equipped herself. It took all of her strength to pull the offending rope through its knot. As soon as Bear could breathe, she rummaged in her small pouch and dug out her lockpick; making quick work of the restraints.

The crowd cried out and moved back as six archers moved in and fanned out across the commons.

The Watch commander pointed his sword through the hole above. "Drop your weapons."

Larina pulled the rope over Bear's head and stood, holding the noose in the air. "Or what? You'll kill us?"

Larina

Not waiting for the commander's response, she threw the noose to the ground beside the discarded manacles and held her hand out to assist Bear to his feet. "You okay?"

Bear was still gasping, but he nodded, rubbing at his neck.

Lozen nodded at Bear and tossed him her dagger, hilt first as she manoeuvred her arrow's aim from one archer to the next.

Bear caught the serrated blade; wrapping his thick fingers around its unique hilt. A smile lifted his pudgy cheeks.

"Unless you can shoot six arrows at once, it's going to be fun trying to get past the Watch," Larina said to Lozen under her breath. "Who *are* you, anyway?"

"Lozen. Elk Warrior. Lozen is not worried."

"Worried or not, you just earned yourself a place of honour up there."

Lozen followed Larina's gaze to the platform. "Lozen won't allow Bolt to hang."

Confused as to where Lozen's loyalties lay, Larina muttered. "Truth be told, I don't relish going back up there either. If they want to string me up, they'll have to kill me first."

"They'll have to go through me first." Bear patted his belly. "This body can absorb a lot of arrows."

The sound of rapid boot-falls descending the platform meant their time was about to run out.

Lozen's eyes narrowed; her bow pointing at the last archer in line who stood with his back to the bay. She indicated the man with a nod of her head. "We go this way."

The archers surrounding them drew their arrows tighter.

Metal boots rang off the cobblestones as dozens of guards moved in to surround them.

Lozen drew her arrow taut. "Ready?"

Larina

Larina wasn't about to give in without a fight, but she knew enough to realize they wouldn't get two steps before they were taken down. Even that prospect didn't bother her as much as it should. The thought of *surviving* the onslaught, did. She refused to allow her injured body to be dragged back up to the gallows for the amusement of the insensitive citizens of Storms End.

Holding her dagger before her didn't instill her with much confidence to fend off the well-armed Watch. A wry smile crossed her lips. Allard's words haunted her: *'Promise me you'll get yourself a better weapon. A dagger's fine if all you want to do is sneak up behind someone and cut their neck, but with the enemies you're acquiring, it won't be enough to keep you safe.'*

The old bugger had been right all along.

She took a deep breath. They had nothing to lose. If they ran hard before the arriving swordsmen had a chance to surround them, perhaps one of them might escape to fight another day.

"Ready."

Larina

Banebridge

"I'll not warn you again. Drop your weapons," the commander ordered. He disappeared from the hole—his steps sounding overhead as he moved to the edge of the platform. "If they so much as move, shoot them."

Larina cast an angry glare at where she thought the commander stood above them; Lozen's subtle movements not lost on her.

Lozen released the tension from her bow and scooped up her arrows; stuffing their points into her right boot. With a subtle nod, she indicated it was time to move.

Larina checked to see which archers appeared to have her lined up, and whispered, "You ready, Bear?"

"Um, I don't think we're going that way," Bear said, pointing Lozen's dagger in the direction of the bay.

"Why n—" Larina gaped at a colossus of a man outfitted in a polished brass cuirass who strode into the commons at the head of a delegation of heavily armed men and women clad in matching grey uniforms. They had appeared from beyond the corner of a low building lining the docks. The long hilt of a sword protruded above the huge man's wide shoulders.

Everyone in the commons, citizens and guards alike, turned to watch the largest man Larina had ever laid eyes on enter the fray—seemingly without a care in the world.

A beautiful smile lifted Lozen's cheeks. She lowered her bow. Pulling her nocked arrow from the string, she dropped to a knee. "Master Banebridge."

Though not customary to greet the son of the Master of Storms End in this manner, many of the citizens emulated Lozen.

Bear's face lit up. He had positioned himself between Larina and the archers—an act that wasn't lost on her. His big hands fell on Larina's shoulders. "Look, it's Pollard."

Larina stared at the heavily muscled giant—striking light-blue eyes beneath a full head of short, red-brown hair. Her breath caught in her throat. She had heard of the goliath over the years from different people, including Bear, but nothing had prepared her to see him in person. She couldn't imagine a more intimidating warrior.

Smiling at the masses, Pollard wiggled his fingers for them to rise—a tinge of embarrassment coloured his cheeks. He surveyed the strange situation; taking time to examine everything from the gallows to the temple as a dozen of his troops fanned out around him.

"Ah, good," the commander on the platform said. He leaned out to see Larina, Bear and Lozen. "Now you'll meet the justice you deserve."

"What goes on here?" Pollard addressed the man.

"Son of Thoril. As temporary ruler of Storms End, I beseech you to apprehend these people."

"Temporary ruler? What happened?"

"These three," the commander indicated with his sword, "have conspired to kill the baron and a captain of the Watch."

Pollard's heavy brow knit together. He closed the distance between himself and Lozen. "Those are serious allegations. Are you accusing my warrior of this crime?"

"Well, no," the commander sputtered. "Not her, exactly."

"Then what, good man? What is her role in this?"

"She freed that man from the gallows." The commander pointed at Bear. "Lozen has also facilitated the escape of Storms End's most wanted criminal."

Pollard tilted his head; his gaze settling on Larina. "You mean to tell me this girl is the Watch's biggest concern?"

"Aye. She's committed countless crimes against the people, burned the north watchtower to the ground, and assassinated the baron, and Captain Danth Emerald."

Pollard gazed at the blackened structure visible above the buildings lining the bay. Returning his attention to the commander, he asked, "The same Danth Emerald who has been terrorizing the upper tiers with his gang of over-righteous thugs? The same Watch captain who has been operating above the law with the blessing of the baron?"

"Well, I-I…This woman is the Storms End Lightning Bolt. She's eluded us for years."

Pollard cupped his chin in his hand. "Ah, yes. The same person who has dedicated her young life to look after our most respected citizens. Feeding and clothing our elders and less well-to-do." He nodded, his warm eyes turning dark. "The very injustice that drove me to leave Storms End. I find your accusations troubling."

The commander of the Watch stared hard at Pollard, his face reddening. "You have no jurisdiction here, son of Thoril. Either help us bring these criminals to justice or be on your way."

Pollard glared back but the commander didn't flinch.

With practised ease, Pollard reached behind his head and pulled his weapon free of its double baldric.

Larina

Larina gaped. The hilt was longer than her forearm. Attached above the guard, two separate sword blades glinted in the afternoon sunshine.

Pollard's corded forearms and bulging biceps brandished the beast of a weapon. Waggling it toward the Watch commander, he declared, "*This* gives me jurisdiction. Have your people stand down until I have time to sort this out."

To his credit, the commander stood firm. "I most certainly will not. You forget yourself, son of Thoril. With the baron's death, I command the Watch *and* the city."

Bear nudged Larina and whispered, "Be ready. Pollard doesn't suffer fools."

Pollard took two measured breaths, stretched his neck, and threw back massive shoulders. "It is *you* who have forgotten his role. In the absence of the baron, the Master of the council is in charge of the city."

The commander made a show of scanning the commons. "Thoril's not here. Therefore, it's my duty to act in his place. If you insist on siding with murderers, I will be left with no choice but to condemn you as an accomplice."

The crowd gasped.

The sound of Pollard's troops baring steel and stringing bows echoed off the temple.

"If you're man enough, commander, why don't you come down here and arrest me yourself?" Pollard glanced over his shoulder and said something to his troops.

As Pollard returned his gaze to the commander, Larina noted his troops shifting into distinct combat formations. She adjusted her sweaty grip on her dagger. Something big was about to happen.

"I didn't think you had it in you." Pollard's eyes scanned the positions of the Watch who had assembled around the gallows in knots of swordsmen and supporting archers—

their numbers bolstered by new arrivals marching down the many streets and converging on the commons. "Typical of those trained under Danth Emerald. Have someone else do your dirty work."

The commander's face reddened. "This doesn't concern you." He gestured to the ranks of the Watch. "You're surrounded and outnumbered. We're not afraid to engage, if that's your choice. Now, do the sensible thing and have your people stand down and let us go about our duty. I'm willing to forget this minor disagreement ever happened."

"I don't wish to be responsible for spilling the blood of the citizens of Storms End." Pollard raised his voice to be heard by the masses. "But neither can I standby and allow a grave injustice to be perpetrated here today. The people who stand condemned before the commander of the Watch are residents of Storms End, just like you and me. Perhaps their actions were harsh, but given the history of the present Watch commanders and the baron, I can only imagine they were left with no choice. People are dying in the streets. *Our* people. Many by the hands of those sworn to protect them. In the spirit of benevolent King Malcolm, I beseech you to disperse and not get caught up in what's about to transpire."

An eerie silence settled over the commons. A cold breeze blew in off the bay, ruffling hair and playing with the hems of tunics and cloaks. The odd cough sounded from different quarters, but no one spoke—their rapt gazes bouncing from the Watch, to Pollard's troops, to the three people at the centre of the stand-off.

Larina's muscles ached with tension—ready to spring as soon as the first blow was exchanged. She scanned the commons, shocked by how many of the Watch had arrived since this whole affair had started at the temple. As much as she appreciated how strong Pollard and his troops might prove, there was no way they could withstand the sheer number of those who stood against them. If the citizens decided to get involved, as often was the case, the resulting mayhem would turn into a bloodbath.

A strange sound drifted over the commons, catching everyone's attention. A murmur rippled through the crowd as everyone started looking around.

At first, Larina couldn't identify where it came from. The rhythmic sound of what could only be described as metallic drumbeats echoed off the cliffs; filling the bay area.

The commander on the gallows' platform pointed his sword at Pollard. "What devilry is this?"

Pollard shrugged; his troops' faces displaying the same bewilderment as everyone else.

Lozen pointed to the street-lined hill above the temple's rooftop.

With no apparent sense of order, a parade of people appeared on every street visible, descending from the upper tiers of Storms End. Men and women of all ages, dressed in rags or regular clothing, strutted toward the commons bearing crude weapons—hammering them against makeshift shields of various sizes. Children and dogs darted about the writhing snakes of marching people. It was as if the entire population of Storms End had been roused into action.

The heads of the processions disappeared behind the lower buildings. The chaotic commotion preceding their march reverberated all over the city; reaching a deafening crescendo as they entered the commons and surrounded those already assembled.

Goosebumps riddled Larina's skin. Led by someone clad in black robes, his identity hidden beneath a cowl, the newcomers squeezed in and around the commons' perimeter, outflanking the Watch and Pollard's troops.

Larina

The crowd jostled forward, eliminating the distance they had afforded Larina and her accomplices. She found it increasingly difficult to maintain her position beside Lozen and Bear, fearing she might drown within the sea of humanity.

The procession took a long time to filter down from the heights, but the percussion never let up until the commons and every street bisecting it, including the bridges spanning the canal, could hold no more.

Purple with rage, the commander shouted, "What's the meaning of this?" He searched out Pollard amongst the shoulder to shoulder crowd. "On whose order have you arranged this uprising, Master Banebridge?"

All eyes were on the giant, but a collective gasp thundered off the buildings lining the commons as the figure in black robes mounted the steps leading up to the gallows.

Dozens of guards made to intercept him, but stopped and bowed when they realized who it was.

Bent over and clad in clothes too big for his stooped form, Thoril Banebridge pulled back his hood and shook out long, grey hair.

Whispers of, "Old man Banebridge," "Council Master," "Half-hand," and many other names swept across the masses.

Larina followed tens of thousands of eyes to the diminutive man ambling across the foreboding structure to confront the commander.

In a stern voice belying his frailness, Thoril declared, "On my order, commander."

The commander stuttered, flabbergasted. "M-Master Banebridge? To what do we owe the honour?"

"Save it, commander. You've done enough damage. Have your men stand down at once."

Larina

Larina feared the commander might toss Thoril from the platform.

Thoril narrowed his eyes. “Now commander, or should I allow the true citizens of Storms End to have their way?”

Moving through the crowd like a four-masted brig breaking heavy seas, Pollard made his way to the gallows and mounted the steps four at a time. The members of the Watch assembled on the gallows stepped back to allow him access. He moved in behind his father and crossed his massive arms—clutching his mighty weapon in one hand.

The commander’s face trembled with outrage. Glaring from father to son, and then over the crowd, he shook his head and stormed away.

Larina

Songsbirthian Guard

Banebridge Manor hadn't seen such a crowd as the one that stuffed the household and sprawled across the manicured lawn at the top of Thunderhead Fjord since the days of Thoril the Kraidic Crusher. Pollard's late grandfather had been larger than life—always living as if it were his last day.

Pollard's father, Thoril Half-Hand, had learned there was more than one way to be an effective leader—preferring to rely on common-sense and diplomacy as compared to the Kraidic Crusher's philosophy that only a dead enemy was a good enemy.

Larina's cheeks hurt. Standing by the same balcony doors she had used her lock pick on, she didn't think she had smiled as much in her entire life. She had been escorted like a heroine from the tense events down by the gallows—up the streets in a raucous celebration of the city's newfound freedom.

Many people, both young and old, thanked her for her unselfish acts over the years; regaling her with their version of tales that concerned her battle with the deposed regime. They had relished the rumours of her exploits—many expressing they had secretly admired her from afar; knowing full well that if their feelings were ever exposed, they too would have faced the wrath of Danth Emerald's Watch.

Larina

Seeing Bear surrounded by so many well-wishers did her heart glad. Her old friend deserved so much better than what life had given him. He had a heart of gold and a level head on his shoulders.

Her eyes misted up watching his sweet face. He deserved someone to love. Someone who could give him all of their love in return. Someone other than her. His feelings for her were more than she was willing to give. Bear was like the brother she never had. Someone to protect her from those intent on harming her. Someone whose shoulder she could cry on and share her most intimate secrets without fear of judgement. Now that the serious issues of Storms End were in better hands, she decided it was time for her to move on. Her father wasn't coming for her anytime soon.

Invited back to Banebridge Manor to celebrate the new regime, it wasn't often that someone wasn't falling over themselves to bestow their gratitude to her. She feared her arm might fall off her shoulder if one more person insisted on shaking her hand.

Enjoying a brief respite, she noted that the smoked-glass dome that had sat on a side table had been removed. Her gaze fell on Pollard and his father patiently speaking with the people of Storms End, no matter their station. The two men ensured that they gave as much attention to the poorly clad men and women who had fallen through the cracks as they did the well-dressed, sophisticated council members. They treated everyone equally and vowed to set things right in the wake of the city's new hierarchy.

The gleam in Thoril's eyes had replaced the tired look she remembered from her brief encounter with him in this very room. He caught her staring.

Graciously excusing himself from the people around him, he joined Larina at the balcony door. “Come, let’s get some air.”

Larina smiled, and opened the door, allowing Thoril to go first. Closing the door behind her, she smiled as he took her arm like a gentleman and led her to the far end of the expansive balcony where they could gaze out upon the back of the large property.

“Looks so much prettier in the daylight,” Larina mused.

“I’ll bet getting through the balcony door was a tad easier this time.”

Alarmed by the comment, Larina stared into his light-blue eyes. She could see where Pollard came by his colouring. It took a moment before Thoril smiled; easing her tension.

“Not much, but yes.” She laughed self-consciously.

Though she was sure his smile was genuine, she detected a reservation toward her. She tilted her head. The man had asked her out on the balcony for a reason. Impatient, she asked, “Any word of Korwynn?”

Thoril shook his head. “Gone. There were reports of a sleek vessel slipping out of the bay shortly after the incident in the commons. If they were Kraidic warriors as I suspect, they’ll be far out to sea by now.”

She nodded and waited for him to get to the point.

He patted her hand and released her arm to lean on the stone railing. When he spoke, it was as if he addressed the sculpted shrubbery. “Before I ask a boon of you, I must know something.”

Unseen by the elder Banebridge, Larina swallowed. “Sure, Master Banebridge. Anything.”

He remained silent for so long she started to wonder whether he had forgotten what he was going to say. When he spoke, his words shocked her. “If things hadn’t gone as badly as they did this morning, would you have given the scroll to the man who called himself Korwynn?"

"I, um…" She knew what she should say, but something about the old man's sincerity prevented her from lying. She whispered, ashamed. "I don't know. Probably."

Thoril nodded. He gave her a measured look and walked away—disappearing into the manor without another word.

Larina stared after him, wanting to explain herself but couldn't. Truth be told, she would have given the scroll to Korwynn in a heartbeat had she been given the opportunity.

She leaned on the railing and stared vacantly across the lawn to where the lichen covered wall marked the property's boundary. She had devoted her life to looking after people who couldn't do so themselves. Now she had to live with the burden of having willingly almost plunged Zephyr into a war it could not win.

She grimaced. How was she to have known the seriousness of the contents of the Crusher Scroll? True, Thoril had tried to warn her, but at the time, her friends' lives were in peril. She sighed. If she had to do it all over, she *would* do it again.

"You sure cause quite a stir."

Larina jumped and spun, dagger in hand. Staring up at the beaming countenance of Thoril's son, she gaped.

"Whoa. Take it easy on me." Pollard stepped back; hands up.

"You scared the death right out of me."

Pollard lowered his hands and moved to the railing. "That's a good thing, is it not?"

"I guess." Larina put her dagger away and joined him, resting her forearms on the railing.

Pollard chuckled. "You guess? Surely you don't wish to die."

She looked up into his warm gaze; raising her eyebrows and feigning a smile, but said nothing.

"Father says you're an interesting specimen."

She frowned at his chiselled profile but he didn't meet her gaze. "A specimen now, am I?"

"His words, not mine."

"Ya, well, I'm surprised he doesn't call me worse," she muttered to the wind.

An uncomfortable silence settled between them. She expected Pollard to berate her for stealing the scroll but he didn't.

A shrill whistle drew her attention to the ancient maple she had used to access the balcony. The Indian woman, Lozen, stood on the meandering pathway with an arm held away from her body; her eyes on the sky over the western wall.

It took Larina a moment to see what Lozen was looking at. The sun at its back, the falcon that had intercepted the scroll on the gallows dropped out of the sky like a black teardrop fired from a crossbow. It opened its swept back wings and extended its talons; alighting on Lozen's arm with practised ease.

"An amazing bird, that one," Pollard said.

"Falcons are incredible birds of prey."

"I was talking about Lozen."

Puzzled, Larina caught the mischief in his eyes and let out a nervous laugh.

"I'm kidding. I have the utmost respect for my warrior friend. She's the finest archer I know. Probably better than Rook Bowman ever was, *or* the Gritian Enervator, Avarick Thwart."

"That's nice." Larina had no idea who those people were, nor did she care.

She couldn't help wonder what Thoril *really* thought of her. As strange as it seemed, the old man's opinion was more important to her than she thought. "Say. If Lozen is *your* warrior, how come she was in Storms End before you?"

"She came ahead on my order."

Larina nodded.

"I sent her to speak with my father about identifying worthy candidates to join me in Songsbirth."

Though she had heard of the place, she had no idea where Songsbirth was located. She'd never been anywhere but Storms End.

Watching Lozen, she had to ask, "Is that why you worked with the Watch?"

Pollard's brow lifted. "Yes, and no."

"Well that sums it up quite nicely. Thanks."

"Hah! It's true what they say. You're a spirited one."

She faked a smile. "I don't do well with people who don't speak straight with me."

"I can appreciate that. To answer your question, straight wise, Lozen accompanied the Watch—Danth, actually—on my father's request."

"Ah. To watch him."

"Um, no, actually…To watch you."

Larina spun on him. "Me?"

"Aye. Apparently when Lozen asked him about worthy recruits, your name was the first to escape his lips…Larina."

She gaped and then nodded, recalling her conversation with Thoril about Allard.

"Aye. With the current atmosphere in the council and the heightened angst of the Watch with regard to your activities, he feared you might not survive until I got here."

"She tried to kill me. Twice."

His handsome smile grew wider. “Believe me. If Lozen wanted to kill you, we wouldn’t be having this conversation.”

“That’s what she said.”

He nodded. “Lozen’s word is her bond. She’s a warrior in every sense of the word.” He gazed at the woman on the lawn. “I wouldn’t want to go against her.”

Larina sized him up and changed the subject. “How tall are you?”

“Eight-foot-three. Eight-five if I stand straight and stretch.”

“My friend, Bear, says you’re a giant.”

He bobbed his head. “Ah. You’re talking about Gom Haulkins. I love that man. A true friend.”

Goosebumps riddled her skin hearing that someone else appreciated Bear.

“I’m actually a half-giant. My mother is…was a giant.” His voice lost its happy lilt. “It’s been over twenty years now since she left us.”

“I’m sorry. What happened, if I may ask? I don’t know much about these things but I thought giants were long lived. Like those pointy-eared creatures.”

“Ah yes, elves.” Pollard chuckled despite his melancholy. “Giants are indeed long lived. Not as long as elves or dwarfs, but much longer than humans.”

Larina thought she detected his eyes moistening.

He looked away. “Helleden happened. My mother died protecting me when I was a wee lad.”

Larina resisted a sudden urge to hug him. She remained respectfully quiet, and followed Lozen’s progress toward the rear of the yard. Where the falcon had gotten to, she had no idea.

“She speaks highly of you.”

Larina frowned. “Huh?”

“Lozen.” Pollard nodded toward the Indian. “Says you would make a fine warrior.”

“Me? A warrior? I doubt it. At least not in Storms End. I believe I’ve worn out my welcome here.”

“Oh, I don’t know about that. But you’re right. I don’t mean in Storms End.” He raised his eyebrows. “Though, the Watch *is* looking for good people now that this is over.”

“Pfft. Like that would go over well.” She dropped her forearms dejectedly onto the railing and faced the backyard. She mimicked two different voices having a conversation. “Oh, look. Here comes the woman who burned down the watchtower.” “Oh, isn’t she the one who slew the captain?”

“I see your point.” Pollard settled in beside her. “Don’t forget,” he raised his voice to a high, squeaky pitch, “Isn’t that the woman who disembowelled the baron?”

Larina gaped but his broad smile made her laugh. “Ya. My days here are numbered.”

“Which brings me to my point.”

Larina held his gaze, thinking to herself, *‘Here it comes.’*

“Would you consider joining the Songsbirthian Guard? It’s a far cry from the Royal Guard, but I believe someone like you would thrive there. Father says you’d make an excellent addition to my team.”

She gave him a skeptical look. “Have you talked to him lately?”

“Yes, actually. Just before I came out here.”

She frowned, recalling how the Master had left her. “Are you sure? I don’t believe he thinks too highly of me.”

“Hmm? That’s strange. He came in and pointed at you, saying, ‘Grab her quick, before she gets away.’ Something about me being able to believe anything you tell me, no matter the gravity.’”

Her frown deepened.

Pollard laughed and shrugged. "Don't ask me. I'm a simple man. The ways of the wise makes my head spin."

She nodded and leaned on the railing. Lozen had walked around the rear of the manor and out of sight. Contemplating Thoril's words calmed her roiling emotions.

Feeling Pollard settle in beside her, she asked without looking at him, "So what now?"

He didn't respond at first. His voice sounded leagues away. "Father senses a dark storm brewing on the horizon. He has asked me to gather a few vital personnel to augment our garrison at Songsbirth."

She felt his eyes on her and turned her head to hold his stare.

"Given the proper training, he believes you will become someone to be reckoned with." He smiled for her benefit. "Coming from Thoril Half-Hand, that's a high compliment. He doesn't bestow praise like that very often, trust me."

"If I agree to accompany you, what are our next steps? Are there more people in Storms End you wish to recruit?" She thought of Bear.

Pollard held her gaze for a while before staring out over the gardens. It was as if he had read her mind. "No. As much as I would like Gom to accompany us, Father says he's needed here. Apparently, Father has plans for Gom that include the council."

Larina thought about that and nodded. Bear *would* make an excellent member of the Storms End wise council. "So then, what?"

"We sail tomorrow to Thunderhead. The port city is vast." He turned his massive frame to look at her directly. "If we're lucky, I might be able to find another Lightning Bolt."

Larina twisted her neck to meet his sincere gaze and smiled. “Pfft. That’ll be the day.” But the happiness she should be feeling wouldn’t come.

Many wonderful people had died as a result of the Watch’s tyranny. The recent backlash a direct result of her brazen actions. She wasn’t sure she’d ever be truly happy again.

Suppressing her urge to cry for Allard, Rock, and everyone else who hadn’t deserved such a cruel fate, she remembered the need to retrieve their bodies. She wouldn’t leave until she properly buried them in the moors above Thunderhead Fjord.

She studied Pollard’s daunting physique and cleared her throat. “Do you mind if I ask a favour before we leave?”

He regarded her with compassion. “Of course. As long as it’s in my power, it’ll be done.”

Larina

To Catch a Tiger

Thunderhead unfolded along the northern shore of Thunderhead Fjord as the *Crusher* sailed into the sun; rounding the waterway's last bend before it emptied into the Niad Ocean.

Rising grey and dull, without any sense of uniformity, Thunderhead sprawled as far as the eye could see to the coast, and north into the foothills of the mountains dominating the region.

Larina stood on the bow with Lozen by her side, admiring the woman's falcon. It sat upon a leather vambrace that protected the woman's forearm; a finely tooled leather hood covering its head.

Pollard stood on the quarterdeck at the stern of the ship, speaking with the helmsman, and captain of the *Crusher*.

As big as Storms End was, Larina wasn't prepared for the sheer size of Thunderhead. Shipyard after busy shipyard lined the fjord, seemingly stretching on without end until the fjord gave way to the sea. Men and women of all sizes and colours worked the docks—a small army of glistening muscle and sweat.

The *Crusher* pulled into a heavily guarded slip amongst three formidable warships. Lozen explained the banners snapping in the wind, high atop the warships' masts, were those of Madrigail Bay.

Larina

Pollard ran down the steep staircase fronting the quarterdeck and emitted a shrill whistle. Several men and women formed up around him.

Lozen removed the falcon's hood and lifted her forearm. She leaned in close to the bird and whispered, "Go. But watch."

The Falcon blinked twice, as if considering her words. With a powerful leap it was airborne and winging away.

Dockworkers stopped to watch it fly inland, over the city, and out of sight.

Larina followed its flight as well until Lozen nudged her in the ribs and rolled her eyes with a playful smile. "Come. Master beckons. We best not keep him waiting. Master gets grouchy."

Larina hurried after her. "Where're we going?"

"To find another Lightning Bolt to train."

"Another Lightning Bolt?" Larina was indignant. Pollard had said the same thing last evening. "Hah. Not likely. There'll only ever be one of me."

Without looking back, Lozen said, "That's what Lozen said. You know how men are."

It didn't take Larina long to realize that Pollard was a man of action. When something needed to be done, he did it. He did it well, and he did it with efficiency. Watching the man operate amongst his troops, there was no doubting why he was the third in command of the Songsbirthian Guard. A position, she had learned since boarding the *Crusher*, that was highly esteemed across the realm. It was all she and Lozen could do to catch up with the small contingent hustling down the jetty and making their way up an alley into town.

Lozen had explained that Zephyr was such a vast kingdom that the kings of long ago had designated three ruling bodies to assist with the daily governance of the land. The court at Castle Svelte was the true governing body, but the monarchs had come to rely heavily on the wise councils of the Chamber of the Wise in Gritian, far to the south, and the Songsbirthian Council, cloistered in the virtually unreachable hamlet of Songsbirth. The Songsbirthian Guard were entrusted to keep the passage to Songsbirth a secret.

Larina and Lozen burst from the far end of the alley, nearly running headlong into Pollard's broad backside. The giant, resplendent in his brass cuirass, stood with his arms crossed and his head nodding.

Larina was taller than most, but she had to stand on her toes to see what was so enthralling.

A large crowd had gathered; the people shouting encouragement and jibes at four combatants squaring off in the middle of what appeared to be a marketplace judging by the tables and tents displaying all sorts of wares.

Forcing her way to the front of the crowd, she watched as two men clad only in tan, leather breeks, held an auburn-haired woman by the arms.

A bare-chested, husky man, wearing the same coloured breeks as the others, held what appeared to be a table leg in his hands and taunted the young woman.

Bouncing on the balls of a pair of knee-high boots, the woman's storm-grey eyes glared hatred at the man; gnashing her teeth and spitting—kicking out whenever he got near.

Larina glanced at Pollard's enrapt stare. "We've got to help her. They'll rip her apart."

Pollard never took his gaze from the fight, but his tone was firm. "Nay, lass. This is not our fight. I have a feeling those poor men are about to find out what happens to people who try to catch a tiger."

Larina frowned, but heeded his words.

Larina

The young woman's skin glistened with sweat as she fought to free herself from her captors' grasp.

The man with the table leg moved in to take a swing, but dodged back again, nearly eating the toe of her boot.

"Hold her steady, damn you!" The man growled at his companions who were struggling to maintain their grip.

The man with the table leg had no sooner spoken than the growling woman bit one man's hand and pulled free of his grasp. Spinning on the other man, her arm twisted painfully in his grasp. Not seeming to care about her discomfort, she kicked him between the legs, not once, but twice.

The second man released her and doubled over in agony, only to receive a third kick to the face that straightened him out and drove him backward to land in a heap.

The man nursing a bleeding arm where her teeth had taken a chunk out of him, ran at her, cursing. His eyes opened wide—trying to get out of harm's way as he spotted the knife in her hand.

The woman stepped into her lunge and drove the knife up and underneath the man's ribs.

An agonized gasp escaped his lips. He fell to the ground clutching his stomach and writhing in pain.

The woman wasted no time turning wild eyes on the one holding the table leg.

The man looked from one of his companions to the other, his mouth open in shock. He held up his hands in surrender, the table leg slipping through his fingers and clattering on the cobblestones.

The woman searched the crowd, adjusting her bladed stance one way and then another, as if daring anyone else to come at her.

"Hah, hah, hah!"

Larina

Pollard's throaty laugh made Larina look up at the wide grin splitting his face. He pointed to the woman glaring death at the crowd. "She's the one!"

He placed a huge mitt on Larina's shoulder. "You two are going to make a mighty fine fighting pair."

Larina frowned in disgust. *'Not bloody likely.'*

The End

Of part one of the Banebridge Companion novels.
The story continues in part two: Sadyra

Thank you for reading *Larina*. I'd be grateful if you would take a moment to leave a review.

If you liked this book, you may also enjoy:

LEGENDS OF THE LURKER SERIES
Reecah's Flight, Book 1
Reecah's Gift, Book 2
Reecah's Legacy, Book 3
Save and buy the Box-set

SOUL FORGE SAGA
Soul Forge, Book 1
Wizard of the North, Book 2
Into the Madness, Book 3
Save and buy the Box-set

I offer personalized, signed, paperback copies, complete with bling!

If you wish to order 1 or more, please check out my website: www.richardhstephens.com

A discount is provided of the purchase on a trilogy.

Sadyra

Chapter one of *Sadyra*: the second book in the Banebridge Companion Novels

Mysterious Cabin on the Hill

There was something mysterious about the cabin on the hill—something sinister, if Sadyra cared to dwell on it. She didn't. She had suffered too many sleepless nights worrying about the rumours whispered in her presence whenever she visited the village of Fishmonger Bay sprawled at the bottom of the hill. The backwater village rife with rumours concerning the shack she called home.

Standing at the end of a path that led away from her family's dilapidated hut, she examined the coastline spread out far below; jagged reefs relentlessly pummeled by ocean swells. Her gaze followed the main trail down a steep slope in the opposite direction of Fishmonger Bay to where it connected with the shoreline and continued northward beneath a promontory of black rock projecting over the ocean at a dizzying height. The Summoning Stone.

She shivered. There was something ominous about that large, flat rock. Perhaps its name. Why would anyone summon anything out there? If there was a place in Zephyr farther away from meaningful civilization, she didn't know of one.

And yet, every three years during the spring equinox, people migrated to the Summoning Stone to take part in a bizarre celebration known as the Mating Festival.

Sadyra

Mesmerized by the relentless waves crashing against the reef, Sadyra shivered. It was high summer, two years after the last gathering, and already she had witnessed the heightened activity surrounding next year's festivities.

She cringed. The hedonistic rituals performed during the weeklong Mating Festival had always repulsed her. Ever since she could remember, her parents had dragged her and her younger sisters to watch the barbaric rituals unfold—all in some bizarre act to appease the dragon gods. Every festival except the last.

The Mating Festival was a time of coming together for the hardy people eking out a meagre living on the rugged shores of the Niad Ocean. Fishermen mostly. The dangerous shoals abutting the coastline around Fishmonger Bay provided those tough enough to live here an abundant supply of fish with which to trade in larger cities like Thunderhead and Storms End, many leagues to the south.

For most of its residents, Fishmonger Bay provided a haven from society—harbouring those seeking refuge from people who might take exception to their past deeds should they ever run into them again.

To Sadyra, the backwater village was a dead-end place to live. Unless, of course, one was content to work themselves from sunup to sundown, breaking their back in hopes of reaping the puny rewards their catch might net them from the skinflint buyers in the big city. Not to mention the ever-present danger of plying one's trade along the razor-sharp reefs lining the northwestern coast of Zephyr. A danger Sadyra was all too familiar with.

Many were the evenings Sadyra's father would stumble into their hut, stone drunk and babbling about the latest victim of the surf. Those days were mostly behind him now. It was Sadyra's turn to brave the unpredictable ocean currents and provide for the household—allowing him and her mother more time to maintain their constant state of semi-consciousness.

Sadyra

Brought up to be a hard worker, Sadyra had done as she had been instructed for as long as she could remember; mending nets, gutting fish, and hauling backbreaking buckets laden with the day's catch from her father's leaky dory to the warehouse fronting the rickety pier. She had learned the value of a hard day's effort, and the daily routine had conditioned her to maintain the rigours of working on the ocean.

Being the eldest child, Sadyra knew nothing else. Up before dawn; expected to prepare breakfast—one her parents would inevitably complain about—and then off to the village to assist her father. Day in and day out, she lugged the family's scant fishing gear down the steep trail into Fishmonger Bay, to where their poor excuse of a boat lay on the gravelly beach.

Every now and then, as they worked the ocean swells, the miserable man would look at her and grumble something about a reckoning. She had no idea what that meant but judging by his scowl, whatever it was, it had to be her fault.

A hand clamped on her shoulder. "Nice view."

Sadyra jumped and reached for the filleting knife tucked in its worn sheath at her waist but the hand stayed her arm.

She swallowed, knowing the voice all too well. Bano Shell. The young man her parents had betrothed her to in the spring. The man with whom she would be expected to take part in next year's Mating Festival.

Sadyra cursed the day she had, in her mother's words, blossomed. At seventeen, her womanly physique had filled out quicker than other girls her age; making her popular with the boys. An attribute she wasn't keen on. Other than her wish to someday get out from underneath the life sucking pall of her parents, she wanted nothing more than to be left alone.

The advent of Bano Shell's betrothal had gone a long way to keeping other suitors away, but Sadyra wasn't convinced that was a good thing.

Faking a smile; dimples lifted her freckled cheeks. “It’s beautiful.”

“I’d say.”

She sighed. Bano’s eyes weren’t looking at the scenery. Shrugging free of his grasp, she waited until his dull, brown gaze met hers.

He raised his eyebrows suggestively. “Tural give you the day off?”

“Couldn’t drag himself out of bed, more like.”

“Again?”

“What else is new?”

“I guess it’s no big deal. You’re running the boat on your own most days now, aren’t you?”

“Pretty much.” She looked away. Her voice dropped to a whisper. “I hit a reef yesterday.”

“Oh, oh.”

She nodded. “Capsized, too. Had to swim it back to shore.”

“Much damage?”

“I’ll say. That’s why I’m standing here. I need Father’s help to fix it.”

Bano looked up the path leading to Sadyra’s hut and said under his breath, “Lose much?”

“The whole lot.”

“And?”

Sadyra fought off tears. She pulled the waistband of her breeks down her hip and lifted her shift part way up her back, exposing a series of deep bruises.

“From the shoals?”

Sadyra shook her head.

“Oh Sadie. I’m sorry.”

Sadyra swallowed. Steeling her emotions, she stared at the raging surf breaking over the reefs far below. She didn’t appreciate Bano calling her by her nickname. Only people she considered friends were allowed to call her Sadie. “Ain’t your fault.”

“True, but you shouldn’t get beaten for an act of nature.”

"Ya, try telling him that. He says I need to keep my mind on what I'm about, not where I want to be. If I paid better attention, I would've seen the reef before I struck it."

"The sea was angry yesterday. You had no business being out there. My father spent the day tending his nets."

Sadyra grimaced. "Ya? Well, according to *my* father, it's my duty to earn me and my sisters' keep. At least until they're old enough to join me."

"Sleena's old enough. What is she? Twelve?"

"Ten."

"Weren't you fishing with your father before then?"

"Oh, aye. I can remember dragging the buckets across the shore. They were half as big as me."

"Why doesn't she help?"

Sadyra shrugged. "Don't know. Father's got a sweet spot for her."

"What about…?" Bano's brow furrowed.

"Sable?"

"Yes, Sable."

It was useless trying to figure out her parents' motivations. "Who knows? If anything, Father detests Sable more than me."

"Come on. It can't be that bad."

Sadyra glowered at him until he broke eye contact.

He shook his head. "And he hasn't said anything more to you about your ancestors?"

Her breath caught. Her family history was a sore point with her parents, and Bano knew it. He had convinced her to inquire about it a few months ago and she had been beaten unconscious as a result.

She glared at Bano and noticed what appeared to be the hilt of a priceless dagger protruding from an ancient sheath attached to his belt. "Where'd you get that?"

He followed her gaze. "Huh? Oh, that? It's nothing, really. Just something my parents gave me."

"Looks expensive."

"Bah. Appearances can be deceiving."

She thought he seemed embarrassed. "Hmm. Well, anyway, I don't care to discuss my father, okay?"

Bano nodded, letting it go. His gaze lingered on the two small headstones barely visible amongst the undergrowth—their amateurish inscriptions no longer legible.

Shaking her head at the impetuous man's fascination with her family heritage, she sat down on the brink of the steep drop-off to await her father.

The sound of a door squealing and banging made Sadyra cringe. Tural Ors was awake.

Bano had grown bored with Sadyra and returned to the village a while ago. She didn't blame him. She wasn't good company today.

Rising to her feet, she looked at the ground as her father lumbered down the path. Stepping onto the main trail, he grunted and made his way toward Fishmonger Bay.

Sadyra fell in behind, mindful to keep her distance lest her presence awaken his latest irritation with her.

The sleepy village of Fishmonger Bay was built in a small clearing at the base of Peril's Peak—the mountain's permanently snow-capped summit sparkling in the afternoon sunshine.

She had climbed those heights on many occasions as a child to escape the wrath of her parents. Two years ago, just before the Mating Festival, she had fled there with her younger sisters to keep them from harm's way. Her parents had indulged in a drunken bender worse than any she could remember. Fearing the outcome, as these episodes never ended well, she snuck Sleena and Sable away from the hut and led them to an abandoned cabin high upon Peril's Peak.

Sadyra

Sadyra had been fourteen then; her sister Sleena, eight, and Sable, five. It wasn't lost on Sadyra that their birth years coincided with the Mating Festival. Nor could she forget the day she had brought her sisters home; weary, starving, and afraid. It had taken her a good month before the resulting injuries of her disobedience allowed her to sleep through the night. It had been a lesson she wouldn't soon forget.

Watching the slumped shoulders of her downtrodden father crunching across the gravel common area between the buildings lining the base of the mountain and the warehouse dominating the shore, Sadyra found herself feeling sorry for him. As much as she hated the sight of the grizzled, pepper-grey haired man, she knew deep down there had to be an underlying reason for his perpetual malaise. One that he blamed her and her sisters for.

Many of the villagers shunned Tural Ors. Upon seeing him, they would change direction and avoid having any dealings with the man. Sadyra had always thought it was largely due to her father's mean streak, but lately she had begun to rethink her views on *both* of her parents' mannerisms.

Feeding on Bano's peculiar interest into her family's past, she started to wonder whether something deeper and darker lie at the root of her parents' troubles. She wished there was someone she could speak to but it was a touchy subject to bring up. It wouldn't end well if her inquiries made it back to her parents. She couldn't afford to spend time recovering if she wished to keep deflecting their everlasting anger from her sisters.

Tural stopped and stared at the damaged boat. Hands on hips, he shook his head and grumbled.

Sadyra couldn't make out what he said, nor did she want to know. Whatever it was, was no doubt directed at her.

She took a deep breath and looked around, hopeful to see other villagers in case he went off. She grunted. Even had there been anyone close by, their presence wouldn't make a difference. Though not the biggest man in the village, she doubted anyone was brave enough to challenge Tural when he was in one of his moods. It was all she could do not to run away as his dark gaze turned on her.

"Where's the rest of the boat?"

She swallowed. The surf pounded the shoreline. Curling waves rose above a ramshackle jetty that extended into the brine. She forced a smile and shrugged, trying to ease the tension with a high-pitched voice. "Out there somewhere?"

Tural followed her gaze. He took a couple of deep breaths. "Your mama's gonna be livid if we don't make this week's quota."

More like, Mama's gonna be angry she can't afford enough grog to keep her pickled, Sadyra thought. Had it been anyone else facing her, she would have voiced her feelings. But not her father. She had enough bruises.

"I reckon you best head into the mountain and fetch us some grub while I see if I can repair this tub."

"Yes, Father."

"It ain't to be pretty, I can tell you that." He shook his head as he examined the damage. "Next time you hit a reef, you best pray your head's between the boat and the rock."

She bit her lips, fighting the angry rebuttal that demanded release; the hurt evident in her soft answer. "Yes, Father."

Bano must have been watching for Sadyra because he caught up to her as she crunched across the commons and slipped between two buildings to gain the trailhead.

"Wait up."

Sadyra stopped, her shoulders stiffening. She rolled her eyes before turning to meet his approach. A forced smile briefly crossed her face. She wanted to be left alone.

"How'd it go?"

She shrugged. "He didn't hit me again, if that's what you're asking?"

"I know. I mean, what did he say?"

So, he *had* been watching. "Not much. Said it was my fault."

She looked toward the ocean swells so Bano wouldn't see her struggling to keep from crying. Her father's words echoed in her mind, *'Next time you hit a reef, you best pray your head's between the boat and the rock.'*

Taking a deep breath, she turned to Bano and lifted her eyebrows. "Father wants me to hunt while he mends the boat."

"I'll grab my bow and go with you."

Not waiting for a reply, he spun around and jogged into the village.

Sadyra sighed but waited for his return.

Bano on her heels, she climbed the foothill to where a smaller path veered toward her family's cabin. She couldn't help but look at the two grave markers hidden amongst the undergrowth. She had never given them much thought before. They had always been there. They were part of the familiar landscape; just as the mountain slope climbing high above their hut, or the dark promontory projecting from the cliffs beyond the foothill.

She took a couple of steps up the side path but Bano's voice stopped her.

"Don't you ever wonder who they were?"

She didn't have to turn around to know who he was talking about. Following his gaze as he crouched and parted the grasses around the granite markers—the eroded inscriptions covered in lichen—he ran a hand over one of the gravestones.

"No. Not really. Father says they were distant relatives from centuries ago."

Bano nodded. "And that doesn't interest you?"

"Why should it? I never knew them."

Sadyra

Bano straightened and faced her, his usual smugness absent. “You do know the history behind the cabin you live in, don’t you?”

Sadyra shrugged. “Ya. Kind of. Don’t really care, to be honest. I’m just counting the days until I can get away from here.”

“I don’t blame you.”

Sadyra thought he was referring to her treatment at the hands of her parents but his next words surprised her.

“A witch used to live in your cabin. A family of them.”

She scrunched her eyebrows. She had heard something to that effect a few times over the years, but hadn’t paid any attention to it. The residents of Fishmonger Bay had nothing better to do once the catch was brought in than tell tall tales of people they had heard about. As a young girl, she had been as frightened by the stories as the next child, but like everything in the forsaken village, nothing was what it seemed. She had had a hard time differentiating truth from folklore until she started hanging out with the older children.

“So I’ve been told.”

“You don’t believe it?”

“Doesn’t matter what I believe. That was a long time ago. It has nothing to do with me.”

“But it does.” Bano’s eyes grew wide. He pointed a dirty fingernail at her. “According to Father Cloth, that hut has been in your family for over five hundred years.”

He nodded as Sadyra frowned.

“Aye. Back to the time of the Dragon Witch.”

Sadyra held his stare and swallowed.

“That means you’re related—”

“Pfft!” Sadyra scowled and stormed up the path. “Doesn’t mean anything. It’s a rumour to scare children into staying off the mountain to save them from the trolls.”

Bano breathed heavily behind her as he tried to keep up—a small hut appearing at the end of the path. “So, you’re calling Father Cloth a liar?”

Sadyra stopped abruptly and spun on him, her finger in *his* face. "I never said that. I said I don't believe what everyone says."

"What? You don't believe in magic?"

The question quenched her rising anger. She took a couple of deep breaths. "I've never met anyone capable of doing anything out of the ordinary. Have you?"

"No but…What about the sorcerer who almost seized the Ivory Throne a couple years back? Surely Queen Quarrnaine didn't give her life to defend the realm from a commoner."

"That's different."

"How?"

"I don't know. Just is. That man came from across the ocean."

"That *man*? His name was Helleden Misenthorpe. People claim he descended from the Wizard of the North."

Sadyra shook her head, tired of the conversation. Bano was speaking in riddles. She had no idea who this northern wizard was, nor did she care. "Whatever. It doesn't matter. Yes, I'll admit there used to be magic users in Zephyr, but from what Father tells me, there aren't anymore."

"Sadyra! What are you doing here? You're supposed to helping your father."

Sadyra rolled her eyes for Bano's benefit and turned to see her mother hanging onto the doorjamb of their one-roomed hut for support. Not even midafternoon and the sour-faced woman was heavy into the spirits.

"It's okay, Mother. Father told me to hunt until he gets it repaired."

Her mother, Areeza Ors, scowled, her weathered face wrinkled well beyond her years. The villagers often remarked how much Sadyra looked like her mother, but Sadyra couldn't see it. She hoped she didn't look anything like the old hag.

Areeza's glassy stare found Bano, as if just realizing he was behind Sadyra. Her face lit up. "Oh! Bano. What a pleasant surprise." Areeza primped her rat's nest—traces of auburn struggling to coexist with mid back length grey strands.

Bano puffed out his chest. "Hi, Mrs. Ors. You're looking swell as ever."

"Och. You're such a flatterer."

Sadyra glared at Bano and said under her breath so only he could hear, "Really?" She shook her head and twisted to slip past her mother into the dingy hut.

Sable and Sleena looked up from the sewing they were doing at the dinner table, their dirty faces following her to the small space the three of them shared at night in the back corner of the cabin on the far side of a cluttered counter.

Retrieving her crude bow hung on a couple of pegs, she found her the protective sleeves for her forearms, snatched up her half empty quiver, and stormed from the hut.

She didn't bother looking at her mother, but Areeza's voice followed her around the back of the cabin, "See to it you get one with meat on it this time. The one you brought back the other day will barely feed a chicken."

Biting back an angry retort, Sadyra stomped across the backyard.

"Sadie, slow down," Bano protested, his gear rattling.

She stopped where the mountainside shot steeply up—its upper heights disappearing beyond an inaccessible ridge—and gave him a dark look. "If you see magic in that woman, you're as drunk as she is."

Candles of varying height flickered around the musty interior of the Ors' family hut—the evening darkness masking the filth and clutter.

Sadyra sat beside her youngest sister, Sable. The skinny whelp nestled into Sadyra's side—more to get away from the sour smell of their mother's breath and her surly looks than to be close to Sadyra.

Sadyra didn't mind. The two shared a special bond. She understood Sable's feelings better than anyone. Other than the times Sadyra took a beating to save her sisters from their parents' wrath, there wasn't an occasion she despised more than gathering for the evening meal.

Sleena sat across the table, minding her own business, but she needn't fear. For the most part, their parents left her alone. Why, Sadyra had no idea. She found herself happy for Sleena and jealous at the same time. Whatever the reason, it wasn't Sleena's fault.

To break the monotonous, brooding silence that gripped every dinnertime, Sadyra said between mouthfuls of venison—part of the catch her mother had complained about earlier. "Do you think there are any magic users left in the world?"

Tural exchanged looks with Areeza before staring hard at Sadyra. "Why do you ask?"

Not sure whether to continue, Sadyra thought, *why not*? It had been Bano's idea anyway, and they loved the cretin.

"I don't know. Something Bano said."

Her parents waited for her to continue.

Sleena stopped eating and watched with interest.

Sable snuggled into Sadyra as if trying to disappear.

Sadyra wrapped a comforting arm around her little sister and examined the slovenly cabin. "Bano said this used to be a witch's hut."

Tural frowned.

"He thinks we might be related to the…" Sadyra swallowed at the dark glares she received from her parents—her last words coming out as no more than a whisper, "…Dragon Witch."

Tural stiffened and stared hard at Sadyra, his face unreadable. Putting down his well-honed knife with the greatest of care, he wiped his lips on his cuff. His chair scraped on the wooden floorboards as he rose to his feet.

Sadyra felt Sable tremble against her.

Sleena bowed her head, not daring to look at either of their parents.

They all knew by their father's mannerism what was about to happen.

"Outside with you," was all he said before he stomped across the hut and threw the door open to the night.

Sadyra looked from Sleena to their mother and sighed. She had the uncanny knack of igniting her father's anger.

Resigned to the fact that she had no choice but to obey, Sadyra swallowed what was left in her mouth, took a sip of water from an old, wooden cup, and followed her father into the darkness.

He waited for her on the end of the rotting porch fronting the hut—its sagging boards in dire need of replacing.

"In the back," Tural grunted.

Not waiting, he disappeared behind the cabin. She contemplated bolting down the path, but she had nowhere to go. The hunting cabin up by the summit was the only place she could think of. Her father would look there first.

She was confident she could get to the old cabin long before he would—a day at least, as she had discovered a back route that no else seemed aware of. That, however, would only intensify the violence her father would hand out. One of these days, she feared he would kill her.

It took every ounce of strength she had to walk down the porch and into the backyard to where Tural waited with hands on hips, refusing to look at her.

She followed his gaze to the full moon—its face partially obscured by a thin veil of cloud.

"What am I to do with you?"

Sadyra didn't trust herself to speak. She interlaced her thin fingers and stared at them clasped together beside the sheath holding her filleting knife.

A dark thought seeped into her mind. It would be too easy to stick him with it. Over and over again until his ridicule and vile ways lay dead at her feet.

She shivered. Where had that come from? She couldn't seriously consider such an action…Could she?

She bit on her lips and forced her gaze to settle on her father's unshaven face. His once chiselled features had sagged over the years—distorted by deep lines and extra weight. Recalling how he looked years ago, she might have considered him handsome once upon a time. But not now. Not with her knowledge of who he really was. A drunken letch who resorted to violence whenever life didn't go as he thought it should. That happened most days now that Sadyra had grown up.

Tural fixed her with that evil glare of his, his dark eyes narrowed beneath heavy brows.

Sadyra flinched and cowered, expecting the inevitable, but Tural crossed thick, hairy forearms on top of his protruding stomach.

"What do you know of magic?"

Surprised, Sadyra gulped, her voice meek. "Nothing, Father. Just what I hear from my friends and Father Cloth."

"Have you felt anything unusual stir inside you?"

Sadyra squinted, trying to find relevance in the odd question. She thought of Bano and felt like spitting. "Not at all. Bano and I have never…" She didn't know how to finish the sentence in an acceptable manner.

"I didn't ask if you were pregnant." Tural tilted his head. "Are you?"

"No!" Sadyra spit out harsher than was wise, but he didn't appear to take exception to her tone.

"That's good. That's the last thing your mother and I need right now."

You and mother? What about me? she thought, but kept it to herself.

He stepped up to her and grabbed her shoulders in his large hands, painfully squeezing as he stared into her eyes. "I mean, have you noticed anything *different* inside? Something weird or foreign to anything you're used to?"

Sadyra swallowed. His grip made her squirm under its pressure but she knew better than to pull away. Wild thoughts raced through her mind as she tried to make sense of his question. "You mean my moon flow?"

He shook her hard—her head whipped back and forth. "No, you dolt! Are you experiencing anything *magical*?"

She couldn't respond until her head stopped shaking. Her scared eyes found his. "No, Father? Why would you ask something like that?"

He shook her again; not as hard this time. "Think! Have you noticed anything out of the ordinary? Like, how you survived the shipwreck when the boat was damaged almost beyond repair? Did you do something a normal person couldn't?"

She remembered the boat being carried on the tidal surges into the reefs. No amount of rowing had been able to avert the water's pull once it had the boat in its clutches. If anything, it was chance that had saved her. Just before the boat hit the shoal, the undertow had exposed the jagged reef. Without thinking, she had jumped over the side of the boat into the heavy surf. The next surge had lifted her over the razor-sharp ridge of stone and deposited her and the remains of the boat on its far side.

"No, Father. I was lucky, I guess. One moment I was rowing for my life, and the next, I was in the water."

His fingers tightened on her shoulders.

She feared he would separate her muscles from the bone. She involuntarily tried to pull away. "Ow! You're hurting me."

He shoved her backward and let go.

She tried to catch herself with several quick backsteps but couldn't help falling on her backside.

Tural stood over her.

She prepared to feel the toe of his boot, but it didn't come.

Tural let out a long breath. "Lucky? Pfft. Weren't lucky for me or your mother."

Sadyra pondered what that meant. She knew all too well that her father would rather she had hit the reef instead of the boat.

He started to walk away but stopped. Without looking back, he said, "If you ever mention the Dragon Witch again, I'll dash your head off the reef myself."

A dark rage festered in Sadyra. She was tempted to get up off the ground and drive her dagger into his back. Gaining her feet, she fought to steady her breathing and glared at his receding form; unabashedly wishing he'd drop dead on the spot.

Her blood ran cold as he stopped at the corner of the hut and turned—shadows casting his features with an evil light.

"You'd best be making up for your mistake tomorrow. Or perhaps you'd rather I put your mongrel to work."

Sadyra's eyes widened. "No. Please. Sable's too young. I'll do better, I promise."

He held her gaze as if searching her soul. "See that you do, else she'll be taking your place, you hear?"

Sadyra swallowed at the inference. If something happened to her, her youngest sister would bear the brunt of their parents' unhappiness. That scared her more than any threat of being beaten.

For some reason Areeza despised Sable almost as much as her. Their father had mentioned Sable looked just like their mother when Areeza was good looking. Before Sadyra had come along and ruined their mother's body.

As her mind returned to the present, she realized her father had gone. Tears dribbled down her cheeks but she didn't care. They fueled her resolve. She would do better tomorrow. Much better. If everything went as she hoped, she could pocket a little coin herself. That was her goal. Work harder than ever before and keep a little for herself—saving it until she had enough to take her sisters away from here. Out of harm's way.

She wasn't concerned about Sleena at the moment, but if she left Sleena behind, their parents would have no one else to vent on. It might do her middle sister some good to see how she and Sable were treated, but in her heart, Sadyra would never do that to her.

She kicked at a half-submerged stone in the grass, dislodging it from a pocket of dirt. Picking it up, she threw it at the back of the cabin; wincing as it almost struck the lone window. If the glass had shattered, so would her body—at the hands of her parents.

Swallowing the bitterness, she trembled with anger at her helplessness. Teeth clenched, she promised herself that someday soon, she and her sisters would be free of the mysterious cabin on the hill. When that happened, she would never go by the family name, Ors, again.

Available now!

Keeper of the Jewel, book 1 in the Highcliff Guardians

Something dark is creeping across the elven kingdom of South March. Something so sinister, that if it is allowed to thrive unchecked, will lead to the end of dragonkind and quite possibly the termination of life as a whole.

The only thing standing in the way of the pervasive evil is a privileged young woman who wants nothing to do with her high standing in life, nor the oppressive responsibilities that accompany the title: Heir to the Willow Throne.

Book 2—Dragon Sect: Coming late 2021

To keep up with everything going on in the Soul Forge Universe, please visit my website at:
www.richardhstephens.com

All books are written within the Soul Forge Universe. There are two, loosely written stand-alone prequels that I published first in order to understand the publishing side of writing. Though loosely written, fans enjoy the back stories of the main characters in the Soul Forge Saga.

The Royal Tournament:

Of Trolls and Evil Things:

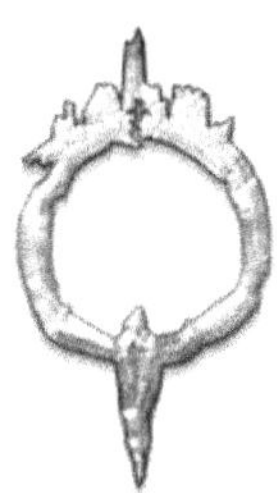

Books by Richard H. Stephens

Soul Forge - The Epic Fantasy Trilogy

Soul Forge – Book 1

Haunted by the murder of his family, a forgotten hero embarks upon a perilous quest fraught with demons both real and imagined.

Silurian Mintaka only wants another drink, but when the people of Zephyr need someone to save them from an evil sorcerer, he agrees to put aside his bitterness and wreak his revenge. Deception, betrayal, and fantastic beasts stand in his way. With the fate of the kingdom in the hands of a homicidal lunatic, the only thing left to do is pray.

Wizard of the North –Book 2

What do you get when you disturb a 500-year-old spirit who is in charge of protecting an ancient magic? A death-defying flight to the heart of a serpent's nest.

If pulling a man through the flames wasn't enough, the highest wizard in the land detonates a thousand years of magical lore.

Not sure whether the king survived the firestorm, the people are left with little choice but to place their trust in a corrupt bishop.

A beast is unleashed and the kingdom's future lies in the hands of an eclectic band of companions who have lost their way.

Can an upstart mage, who isn't what they appear, stand against the evil sweeping the realm?

Into the Madness –Book 3

The epic conclusion of the Soul Forge Saga.

How do you survive a confrontation with a wyrm bent on destroying the world? Walk into its gaping maw and fight it from within.

A ragtag group of assassins set out to end the land's suffering only to discover death awaiting them with open arms.

A carefully hidden truth is revealed—the key to the kingdom's salvation if the Wizard of the North and her unstable companion can live long enough to unlock its secret.

Waylaid by an eccentric necromancer, and suffering a tragic loss that threatens to ruin their poorly laid plan, the companions stagger toward a fate no one ever envisioned.

An obsidian nightmare is summoned and Zephyr will never be the same.

Legends of the Lurker Series

Reecah's Flight –Book 1

Everyone knows dragons are dangerous, but to hunt them is insane.

There is something strange about the woman living on top of the hill and the people of Fishmonger Bay leave her alone. At least until the day she visits the village witch.

Her life spinning out of control, Reecah must decide whether to slay the dragon or risk becoming a victim of her people.

Can Reecah find the key to unlock her family heritage or will she fall prey to the secret so many have died to protect?

Reecah's Gift – Book 2

The appalling mannerisms of those entrusted to protect the kingdom are shocking.

Braving the perils of a cutthroat city isn't what Reecah envisioned when she sought out a better place.
Can a ruthless giant equip her with the skills she needs to confront the king, or will his unorthodox ways end up being the death of her dreams?

Is an alliance with a murderous elf and a sly dwarf the best way to avert the plight of the dragons? And what is this *Gift* everyone seems to know about? Everyone, except Reecah.

Find out how the machinations of the evil prince and a traitorous wizard turn Reecah's quest on its head in this epic, second installment of the Legends of the Lurker.

Reecah's Legacy – Book 3

The culmination of the Legends of the Lurker trilogy.

Reecah Windwalker comes into her own as she finds peace with her past and bravely sets out to fulfill her legacy.

Keeping a promise to a dead witch, Reecah seeks those who can help her learn the ways of her dragon magic as she embarks on a desperate journey to save the last of the dragons from the dark heir.

The races come together, but their combined strength may not be enough to prevent the high king's dragon slayers from eradicating the beauty from the land.

Banebridge Companion Novels

Larina – Book 1

(A story from the Soul Forge Universe)

Growing up on the streets of Storms End, Larina knows the only way to survive is to take matters into her own hands.

Skulking about the seedy alleyways and taverns of a once great city that has fallen from grace, survival has become a game of steal and lie, or die.

Larina uses her ill-begotten abilities to help the vulnerable, less fortunate souls abandoned by life. An act that fills her with a sense of purpose and pride.

That all changes when the man with the black warhammer comes to town. Now the Storms End Lightning Bolt must decide whether those she has fought so hard to protect will be better off if she ends up dead.

Sadyra – Book 2
(A story from the Soul Forge Universe)

Living in the shadows to avoid the brutality of parents harbouring a dark secret, Sadyra must force a violent confrontation if she is to keep her younger sisters from harm's way.

Begrudgingly accepted to work alongside a hardened group of sailors, Sadyra learns how to survive in a ruthless world.

To save her sisters from a fate worse than death, Sadyra goes against everything she feels is right, and life as she knows it will never be the same.

The Royal Tournament

(A story from the Soul Forge Universe)

The Royal Tournament has at long last come to the village of Millsford.

For Javen Milford, a local farm boy, the news couldn't be better. Finally, Javen can perform his chores on the homestead and partake in the biggest military games in the kingdom, hoping beyond hope that just maybe, he might catch the eye of the king.

Javen enters the kingdom's flagship tournament only to discover that in order to win, one must be prepared to die.

Of Trolls and Evil Things

The (standalone) prequel to the Soul Forge Saga series!

Travel down an ever-darkening path where two orphans battle to survive upon a perilous mountainside, evading the predators and prowlers preying upon its slopes, and within its catacombs.

When the dangers they face force them from their mountain home, they end up in the cutthroat streets of Cliff Face plying their hands as beggars to survive.

Strange circumstances spin their lives out of control, forcing them onto the nefarious slopes of Mt. Gloom in a desperate effort to escape the unpleasant reality looming over them; only to discover their worst nightmare awaits them with open arms.

Born in Simcoe, Ontario, in 1965, I began writing circa 1974; a bored child looking for something to while away the long, summertime days. My penchant for reading The Hardy Boys led to an inspiration one sweltering summer afternoon when my best friend and I thought, 'We could write one of those.' And so, I did.

As my reading horizons broadened, so did my writing. Star Wars inspired a 600-page novel about outer space that caught the attention of a special teacher who encouraged me to keep writing.

A trip to a local bookstore saw the proprietor introduce me to Stephen R. Donaldson and Terry Brooks. My writing life was forever changed.

At 17, I left high school to join the working world to support my first son. For the next twenty-two years I worked as a shipper at a local bakery. At the age of 36, I went back to high school to complete my education. After graduating with honours at the age of thirty-nine, I became a member of our local Police Service, and worked for 12 years in the provincial court system.

In early 2017, I retired from the Police Service to pursue my love of writing full-time. With the help and support of my lovely wife Caroline and our five children, I have now realized my boyhood dream.

If you wish to keep up to date on new releases, promotions and giveaways, please subscribe to my newsletter by checking out the contact tab on my website.

www.richardhstephens.com

Facebook: richardhughstephens
Twitter: RHStephens1
Instagram: richard_h_stephens
YouTube: bit.ly/2NKpOhn

www.ingramcontent.com/pod-product-compliance
Ingram Content Group UK Ltd.
Pitfield, Milton Keynes, MK11 3LW, UK
UKHW020143250726
13967UKWH00002B/838

9 781989 257272